P9-BZJ-464

Olivia

THE SMUGGLER'S TREASURE

❧

by
Sarah Masters Buckey

American Girl™

Published by Pleasant Company Publications
© Copyright 1999 by Pleasant Company
All rights reserved. No part of this book may be used or reproduced in
any manner whatsoever without written permission except in the case of
brief quotations embodied in critical articles and reviews.
For information, address: Book Editor, Pleasant Company Publications,
8400 Fairway Place, P.O. Box 620998, Middleton, WI 53562.

Printed in the United States of America.
00 01 02 03 04 RRD 10 9 8 7 6 5 4 3 2

History Mysteries® and American Girl™
are trademarks of Pleasant Company.

PICTURE CREDITS
The following individuals and organizations have generously given permission to
reprint illustrations contained in "A Peek into the Past": p. 155—The Historic New Orleans
Collection, acc. #1947.20; pp. 156-157—*Impressment of Bostonians* by Knowles, North Wind
Picture Archives; Ann S.K. Brown Military Collection, Brown University (White House);
Detail of *Dolley Madison Saving the Declaration of Independence,* CORBIS/Bettmann; pp. 158-159—
The Land of Evangeline by Joseph Rusling Meeker, The Saint Louis Art Museum (Modern Art),
163:1946; CORBIS/Bettmann (Jean Lafitte); The Historic New Orleans Collection, acc. #73-38-L
(flag raising); pp. 160-161—© James R. Lockhart (courtyard); Courtesy, Winterthur Museum
(sampler); Courtesy of the Wenham Museum, Wenham, MA. Photo by Lynton Gardiner (doll).

Cover and Map Illustrations: Troy Howell
Line Art: Greg Dearth
Editor: Peg Ross
Art Direction: Laura Moberly
Design: Tricia Doherty and Laura Moberly

Library of Congress Cataloging-in-Publication Data

Buckey, Sarah Masters, 1955-
The smuggler's treasure / by Sarah Masters Buckey. — 1st ed.
p. cm. — (History mysteries ; 1)
"American girl."
Summary: Sent to live with relatives in New Orleans during the War of 1812,
eleven-year-old Elisabet determines to find a smuggler's treasure
to ransom her imprisoned father.

ISBN 1-56247-813-3 ISBN 1-56247-757-9 (pbk.)
1. Louisiana—History—War of 1812—Juvenile fiction.
[1. Louisiana—History—War of 1812—Fiction. 2. United States—History—War of 1812—
Fiction. 3. New Orleans (La.)—Fiction. 4. Buried treasure—Fiction. 5. Smuggling—Fiction.]
I. American girl (Middleton, Wis.) II. Title. III. Series.
PZ7.B87983 My 1999 [Fic]—dc21 98-47808 CIP AC

In memory of my parents,
Margaret and Parke Masters,
with love and gratitude

TABLE OF CONTENTS

New Orleans

Mississippi River

Barataria

The pirate base
of Barataria

ELISABET'S WORLD
Louisiana in 1814

Gulf of Mexico

British warships

Chapter I
Pirates and Pickpockets

August 28, 1814

Eleven-year-old Elisabet Holder climbed the wooden ladder from the *Marissa*'s dark lower deck to the brilliant sunshine on the top deck. As she poked her head out the open hatch, she could hear the sails snapping in the wind, and a warm, humid breeze blew back her hair.

The air smelled like land. It was not the cool New England smell of pine trees and new-mown hay. This hot, wet land smelled of swamp grasses and rich earth. But it was land all the same. She breathed deeply.

Today I'll finally reach New Orleans! she thought. *If only Papa could be here with me!*

From her perch on the ladder, Elisabet looked at the strange scene around her. The banks of the broad, muddy Mississippi were lined with towering cypress trees, which stood with their knobby roots in the water and their

branches reaching out over the river. Veils of lacy, gray
Spanish moss hung from the branches. When the wind
blew, the trees in their gray veils looked to Elisabet like
thousands of mourners, swaying in time to some far-off
funeral music.

Just across the river, she saw two Indians paddling by
in a canoe-like boat called a *pirogue*. Near the Indians, a
fierce-looking alligator climbed out of the mud and onto
the riverbank. Elisabet shuddered as she watched the huge
alligator snap its jaws at a seagull. It was all so different
from Boston!

Suddenly, she heard a whoop of excitement from the
prow of the ship. "Look, there's the cathedral! Its towers
are there, above the trees," a short, round cotton merchant
called out, pointing off into the distance. "We're not far
from New Orleans now."

Feeling anticipation mixed with dread, Elisabet hurried
over to join the passengers clustered by the railing. She
found a place next to Mr. Robinson, a tall, elegantly
dressed gentleman who had boarded the ship from a
plantation the day before.

He smiled at her. "Well, Elisabet, you've sailed a great
distance. Has the trip been anything like you thought it
would be?"

Elisabet thought for a moment. It had taken six weeks
for the *Marissa* to travel from Boston, down the East
Coast, around Spanish Florida, across the Gulf of Mexico,

and up the Mississippi River. She didn't want to admit how frightened she had been during the roughest parts of the voyage. But she didn't want to lie, either.

Finally she said, "My father always told me that sailing on the seas was a great adventure. But this trip was even more exciting than I'd thought it would be."

Mrs. Murdoch, a thin, sour-faced woman who was standing nearby, scowled. "Exciting!" she exclaimed. "It was awful! Why, with pirates out there and this terrible war going on with the British, I was scared to death every time we saw another ship! And the storms! I declare there were times I thought we'd never see dry land again!"

The cotton merchant nodded. "Remember that night when the winds blew so hard the ship was sailing on its side? We were all sick as dogs."

As Elisabet listened to the older people, she recalled that while she sometimes had been scared during the violent storms, she had never been seasick. *I have a strong stomach,* she thought proudly. *Just like my father.*

Now, however, she felt a knot of fear in her stomach. *What will my aunt and uncle be like?* she wondered as she looked over the ship's railing toward New Orleans. *Will they be glad to see me? Will they help me find Papa?*

"No need to look so worried, Elisabet." Mr. Robinson's soft Southern accent interrupted her thoughts. "We're almost there. Look, the birds have come to escort us into harbor!"

He threw a ship's biscuit to one circling seagull. The bird caught it, then dropped it back onto the *Marissa*. "These birds have good sense, too," he chuckled. "This ship serves the worst food I have ever tasted."

Elisabet laughed, and Mrs. Murdoch, who was standing close by, looked at her disapprovingly. The older woman had been suspicious of Mr. Robinson ever since he had stepped on board. "Look at his fancy clothes," she had whispered to Elisabet. "I'll bet he's one of those no-good New Orleans gamblers. You stay away from him."

Even if he *was* a gambler, Elisabet liked Mr. Robinson. He had a ready smile and the polite manners of a gentle-man. Now he asked, "Who is meeting you in New Orleans, Elisabet?"

"I believe my Uncle Henri and Aunt Augustine will be there," she replied. "My father's lawyer, Mr. Gruber, wrote to them after my father was captured by the British. My uncle wrote back, inviting me to come live with them."

"How well do you know them?"

"Not at all," she admitted. "Uncle Henri is my mother's older brother, but my mother died when I was little. My father rarely spoke about her family."

Mrs. Murdoch leaned toward the cotton merchant. Pointing to Elisabet, she said, "This poor little orphan has lost both her parents. Now she's going to live in New Orleans with an aunt and uncle she's never met."

Elisabet felt her face grow hot with anger. She turned

to Mrs. Murdoch. "Excuse me, ma'am, I'm *not* an orphan. My father is alive—but he's a prisoner of the British. He'll be freed someday, and then we'll be together again."

"How did your father come to be a prisoner?" asked Mr. Robinson sympathetically.

Haltingly, Elisabet explained that the trouble had begun five months ago. Her father had been at sea with his cargo ship, the *Independence,* when he was stopped by a British warship. British officers boarded Captain Holder's ship and examined its valuable cargo of tools and supplies.

Despite Captain Holder's protests, the British officers demanded identification papers for every man aboard. They said they were searching for British sailors who had deserted their country and joined the Americans. When the British checked Captain Holder's papers, they discovered he had been born in London. Although Captain Holder explained that he lived in Boston and was now an American citizen, the officers claimed he was British— and a traitor to the crown. They stripped the *Independence* of its cargo and dragged Captain Holder away in chains.

At this point, Elisabet paused. No matter how many times she told her father's story, it still brought tears to her eyes. But she was determined not to cry. She dug her nails into her palm. "The crew brought my father's empty ship home," she added quietly, "but my father is still a prisoner."

"Don't give up hope," said Mr. Robinson gravely. "Sometimes the British will trade our captured sailors for ransom money. It depends upon how valuable the prisoner is to them."

"I know those British devils have taken some of our best men—and a great deal of cargo, as well," said the cotton merchant. "I myself lost thousands of dollars when they claimed a shipload of my cotton."

"I don't know what they want with our sailors anyway," said Mrs. Murdoch, as she fanned herself briskly. "Don't they have enough of their own?"

"The British have the biggest navy in the world, madam," explained Mr. Robinson. "They always need more sailors to man their ships, especially with the wars they are fighting here and in Europe. If they find a sailor on an American ship who was born in Britain, chances are they'll claim he's British and take him away."

"I hope this accursed war with England ends soon so we can return to business as usual," the cotton merchant grumbled.

"And I hope your father is soon returned to you, too, Elisabet," Mr. Robinson said kindly.

"Thank you, sir," Elisabet replied. She hesitated, then asked, "Have you ever heard of the British ship *Sophie*?"

Mr. Robinson shook his head. "Can't say I have. Why?"

"That's the ship that took my father prisoner. My father's first mate told me it was headed for the Gulf of

Mexico. So perhaps my father's not too far from New Orleans."

"It's possible," Mr. Robinson agreed. "But the Gulf of Mexico is awfully big, and the chance that a British ship will come near New Orleans is awfully small—unless, of course, the British decide to invade us."

A British invasion of New Orleans? Elisabet had never imagined such a thing. "Would the British sail up the Mississippi, just like all these other boats?" she asked.

Mr. Robinson shrugged. "Possibly. But if they wanted to surprise us, they would come through the swamps. It's the most direct route."

"The British would never go through the swamps—only Indians, pirates, and smugglers dare go there," the cotton merchant declared. "The swamps are filled with snakes and alligators. And those creeks called bayous bend every which way. If you take one wrong turn, you're lost forever!"

"It's not easy traveling through the swamps," Mr. Robinson admitted. "But the British could do it if they had a good guide or a detailed map."

"Surely you jest, sir," said Mrs. Murdoch. "Why would the British send their troops through miles of miserable swamps just to reach New Orleans? They could capture many other American cities far more easily."

"Perhaps," Mr. Robinson agreed, as he watched another sailing ship pass along the river. "But how many of those cities have the wealth and beauty of New Orleans? Besides, whoever controls New Orleans controls all the trade along the Mississippi River. That's no small prize."

"Prize, my foot!" Mrs. Murdoch declared scornfully. Her thin mouth hardened into a line. "New Orleans is just a den of thieves and sinners. Why, I hear that no-good Jean Lafitte practically runs the city. His pirates walk the streets in broad daylight!"

Elisabet felt the lump of fear in her stomach grow. Throughout the voyage, Mrs. Murdoch had talked about the danger of pirates. She had said they were bloodthirsty outlaws who thought nothing of murdering men, sinking ships, and throwing children to the sharks.

"Is New Orleans really full of pirates?" Elisabet asked Mr. Robinson.

He turned to her. "With all due respect to Mrs. Murdoch, Jean Lafitte is a privateer, not a pirate. Pirates will attack any ship. Privateers such as Monsieur Lafitte, however, will attack only our enemies, never American ships. In fact, if the British should decide to invade, Lafitte might be our best protection. He and his men know the swamps better than anyone."

"You know an awful lot about pirates, Mr. Robinson," Mrs. Murdoch said suspiciously.

"Privateers," Mr. Robinson corrected her. "They are legitimate businessmen. And yes, I've done business with them."

"Pirates or privateers—what's the difference?" Mrs. Murdoch sniffed. "New Orleans is a sinful city, and I'm glad I shan't be staying there." She turned to Elisabet. "Now, you remember to watch for pickpockets like I told you, and"—she made a pointed glance at Mr. Robinson— "watch out for gamblers, too."

"Yes, ma'am," Elisabet replied, her heart sinking. *Pirates, pickpockets, and gamblers*, she thought. *What kind of place does my uncle live in?*

Mr. Robinson smiled at her and winked. "You'll love New Orleans, Elisabet. It's a jewel of a city. But you should go pack. We'll be landing soon."

CHAPTER **2**

ALONE

Elisabet nodded. She took one last gulp of the land air. Then she climbed back down the ladder and made her way through the narrow, dark passageway that led to the room reserved for women and children. The passageway was so dim she had to grope for the handle of the door.

Inside, light from a small open porthole illuminated the long room, which was lined with narrow bunks. In the center of the room, two immigrant women were packing their belongings in large wooden trunks and chattering in German as babies played around them. The room smelled strongly of dirty diapers. Elisabet tried not to breathe too deeply as she made her way to her bunk.

She took out her small satchel and began packing her things. As she folded a white linen petticoat, she fingered the delicate embroidered flowers on its hem and thought longingly of the home she had left in Boston. Captain

Holder had been one of Boston's most successful citizens, and nothing had been too good for his only child. The Holders' housekeeper, Mrs. Rigsby, had fussed over every detail of Elisabet's dress, making sure her clothing draped perfectly and her silk ribbons were tied just so.

"'Tis only right you should look like a fine young lady," Mrs. Rigsby would tell Elisabet proudly. "After all, aren't you the daughter of the great Captain John Holder?"

But everything had changed for Elisabet after her father was imprisoned and his cargo stolen. Captain Holder's lawyer, Mr. Gruber, had become Elisabet's temporary guardian. He had told Elisabet that her father must repay a great deal of money to the merchants who had owned the stolen cargo.

The lawyer had hastily sold the Holders' house, their land, and almost everything else of value, including Elisabet's favorite books, her beautiful mahogany four-poster bed, and a silver mirror that had once belonged to her mother. All of the Holders' servants were dismissed too, even Mrs. Rigsby.

Then the lawyer had announced that Elisabet must move to New Orleans, to live with her aunt and uncle there.

"I can't leave Boston!" Elisabet had protested. "What if Papa comes back and finds me gone?"

"Your father's not coming back," the grim-faced lawyer had insisted. "You had better face facts. You've no money or family left here in Boston. Your only kin is in

New Orleans. That is where you must go."

Elisabet had been allowed to take only a few sets of clothes for the trip. Now she packed these carefully in her satchel, along with her brush, her small amount of spending money, and her family Bible. Finally, she tucked in her beloved doll, Agnes, the only toy she had been allowed to keep from the many she had once owned.

"We're almost in New Orleans, Agnes," she whispered to the doll. "Soon we'll be on land again."

After she had finished fastening her satchel, Elisabet made her way back down the narrow passageway. She had almost reached the wooden ladder when she met Mrs. Murdoch coming from the top deck.

"I shall not be going ashore with you," Mrs. Murdoch announced. "You recall that I told your guardian I would watch over you during the voyage?" She glanced at Elisabet sharply.

Elisabet nodded, but she recalled how Mrs. Murdoch had actually spent most of the voyage in bed, complaining bitterly of seasickness.

"Well," Mrs. Murdoch continued, "I said nothing about New Orleans. I refuse to set foot in that evil city, and besides, your aunt and uncle will be there to meet you. I'm staying right here until a boat from my husband's plantation comes to fetch me."

"Yes, ma'am," said Elisabet. She did not know whether to feel relieved at seeing the last of Mrs. Murdoch or worried to go ashore by herself. "I understand."

"Of course, you will have an easy time of it," Mrs. Murdoch continued, half to herself. "I expect your aunt and uncle's home there will be as comfortable as your father's—with servants to wait upon your every need."

"Thank you, ma'am," Elisabet said, but she could not imagine any home as wonderful as the one she'd left in Boston. She felt a stab of pain as she remembered how Papa used to walk through the big front door, smiling broadly and opening his arms for a hug. *Without Papa*, she thought, *no place will seem like home.*

Suddenly, Mrs. Murdoch narrowed her eyes and looked at Elisabet's satchel. "Where's the rest of your luggage, child?"

"This is all I brought, ma'am," Elisabet replied reluctantly.

"Tsk, tsk," Mrs. Murdoch clucked. "I guess you won't have to worry much about pickpockets after all." She frowned and seemed to hesitate for a moment. Then she reached into her pocket and pulled out a shiny coin. "Here, child, take this."

Elisabet eyed the coin as if it were a glittering diamond. For a moment she was tempted to take it. She had so little money in her bag! But then she looked up and saw the pity in Mrs. Murdoch's eyes. Her spine stiffened.

"I do not need your money, ma'am," she told Mrs. Murdoch firmly. "I'll be fine."

Holding her satchel tightly under one arm, Elisabet climbed to the upper deck. When she reached the top, she caught her breath. There was New Orleans—less than a quarter of a mile away and getting closer every moment!

Sailing ships, cargo boats, and large log rafts—all were lined up along the levee, a wide embankment of raised land along the riverbank that formed a barrier between the city and the powerful river.

There was little spare room along the busy levee, but the *Marissa*'s captain skillfully steered toward a vacant spot next to another sailing ship. As the ship maneuvered toward land, the crew hurried about the deck to secure the rigging. A small crowd of people on the levee pointed and waved toward the *Marissa*. Many of Elisabet's fellow passengers excitedly waved back and called out to friends onshore.

Elisabet felt suddenly small amid the hurricane of activity. She stood quietly at the edge of the waving passengers and wondered if Uncle Henri and Aunt Augustine were waiting for her somewhere in that blur of people on the levee.

She saw Mr. Robinson walk by carrying his two heavy bags. He stopped in front of Elisabet, put down one of his bags, and rummaged in his pocket. For a moment, Elisabet feared he too would offer her money. But instead of a coin, Mr. Robinson pulled out a cream-colored engraved card and handed it to her.

"Good luck in your new home, Elisabet," he said with a smile. "If you ever need assistance, you may call on me."

"Thank you, sir," Elisabet replied, dropping her best curtsy. She looked at the card:

Jeremiah Robinson, Esq.
Attorney-at-law
Seven Rue du Chevalier
New Orleans

So the man Mrs. Murdoch had accused of being a gambler was actually a lawyer! Elisabet smiled to herself. She did not think she would ever need a lawyer's help, but it was reassuring to have a friend in New Orleans. She tucked the card in her satchel.

Then she felt a thud. The boat had docked, and the next few minutes were a whirl of confusion. Everyone who was getting off in New Orleans gathered by the gangplank. Mr. Robinson was the first in line. By craning her neck, Elisabet could see the lawyer crossing onto shore and being greeted by several well-dressed gentlemen. Then he was swallowed up in the crowd.

Elisabet picked up her satchel and headed down the gangplank. Her heart was pounding, but she tried to look unconcerned, as if arriving in a strange new city were an everyday occurrence for her.

There was a sharp drop at the end of the gangplank where the ramp met the levee. A big sailor with a bandanna over his head stood there, and he swung Elisabet onto the ground as easily as if she were a sack of sugar. As soon as she stepped onto the levee, her legs felt wobbly. After six weeks aboard ship, she had become accustomed to the deck swaying beneath her. Now that she was standing on the ground, she felt as if the whole world were rocking.

All around her, other passengers were being welcomed with hugs and shouts of joy. Elisabet steadied herself and began to look for her aunt and uncle. She saw an attractive couple walking toward her. Her spirits lifted, and she gave them a shy smile. But the couple walked by. Her heart dropped.

Then she saw two fashionably dressed couples approaching. She allowed herself to hope that one of these couples might be Aunt Augustine and Uncle Henri. *If I must live in New Orleans*, she told herself, *it would be nice to have a lovely home and beautiful clothes again.*

Yet these couples also passed her without a second glance. She scanned the faces of everyone—young and old, rich and poor—she thought might possibly be her aunt and uncle. But no one appeared to be searching for a red-haired, eleven-year-old girl.

Elisabet tried to stand tall and proud, just as the daughter of Captain John Holder should. Mindful of Mrs. Murdoch's warnings about pickpockets, she held tight to her satchel, too. Yet as she stood and waited in the sun, her forehead dripped sweat and her long-sleeved, heavy linen dress stuck to her body.

She yearned for a shady place to sit, but she was afraid that if she moved from the levee, her aunt and uncle might never find her. So she continued to wait as people hurried by, talking and calling out in French, Spanish, accented English, and other languages. Stylish young gentlemen paraded along the levee in tight green pantaloons. Pretty girls strolled past in light silk dresses that looked like colorful flowers. Elisabet thought these colors would have been considered much too bright in Boston, but somehow they looked just right under New Orleans' scorching sun. She envied their coolness, too.

Many people, however, were not so well dressed. Elisabet saw dark-skinned laborers in worn breeches, beggars in rags, and Indians who wore hardly any clothes at all. She watched a girl walk by wearing only a thin, faded cotton dress and carrying a big basket of apples on her head. The girl had coffee-colored skin and a tired, mournful expression on her face. Elisabet wondered if she might be a slave. She'd heard about slaves but had never seen any in Boston.

I wish I were back in Boston, Elisabet thought with a wave of homesickness, as she swatted at mosquitoes and tried to fan the hot, humid air from her flushed face.

The sun was going down on the horizon now, painting the western sky a vivid purplish red. The crowds were beginning to thin, too. Still Elisabet saw no sign of anyone who looked remotely the way she imagined her aunt or uncle might look.

She was determined not to cry, but a scared voice inside her kept whispering, *What if nobody comes?*

CHAPTER 3

AN UNEXPECTED INTRODUCTION

Suddenly, Elisabet noticed a dark-haired, barefoot girl about her own age running down the levee. The girl was dressed in a simple blue cotton work shift and a white apron. Elisabet guessed she was a servant or a shop assistant. As she ran, her apron's ribbons flew out behind her.

When the girl neared the *Marissa*, she looked up and down the levee. Then she headed for Elisabet. "I am looking for Elisabet Holder," she announced in French-accented English. "Perhaps you . . ."

Elisabet drew herself up as tall as she could. "I am Miss Elisabet Holder. Do you have a message for me?"

To Elisabet's great surprise, the dark-haired girl smiled and gave her a hug. "*Bonjour*, welcome!" she exclaimed as she planted kisses on both of Elisabet's cheeks. "We are very glad you have come. I am sorry to be late. I only just heard your ship had arrived."

Elisabet pulled back. Why was this servant hugging her? "Who are you?" she asked.

The girl laughed. "Ah, *oui!* I forget to introduce myself. I am Marie. I work in your aunt's bakery. Madame DuMaurier asked me to meet you. She regrets she herself is not able to be here."

Elisabet felt a wave of relief. At least someone had come to meet her. "My aunt and uncle—are they all right?" she asked.

Marie's smile vanished. She looked down at the levee. "I am sorry to bring you bad news," she said. "Monsieur DuMaurier has . . ." She paused and struggled for words. "He passed away."

"That cannot be!" Elisabet exclaimed. "Why, I received a letter from him just before I left Boston! He invited me to come here!"

Marie nodded. "*Oui,* I know. But the good Lord took Monsieur away from us not long after he wrote to you. It was very sudden. Even now it seems hard to believe he is no longer with us. We miss him so much!"

Despite the heat, Elisabet felt a sudden chill. All these weeks, she had been thinking about her uncle, picturing how he might look, imagining how he might greet her.

"I wish I'd known," she said. She was almost afraid to ask her next question. "My Aunt Augustine, is she well?"

"*Oui!*" Marie reassured her. "But she had to travel to Baton Rouge three weeks ago. Her daughter, she is married to a shopkeeper there and has been very ill." Marie dug into her skirt pocket and pulled out a folded paper. "Here, Madame left this for you."

Leaning back against a stack of cotton bales piled on the levee, Elisabet unfolded the note with trembling fingers.

The Sixth of August, 1814

My Dear Elisabet,

So much has happened since my beloved husband wrote to you! He was the best and kindest of men. I miss him terribly, but I am comforted by the knowledge that he is now in Heaven.

I had greatly wished to welcome you in person, but unfortunately my duties as a mother call me to Baton Rouge. My daughter by my first marriage lives there and is desperately ill. I am hopeful that a mother's tender care will help her recover. I shall return home as soon as she is well.

While I am away, Marie will teach you how to work in the bakery. Despite all the sadness of recent days, I am glad you have come to New Orleans, my dear. Your help in the bakery will be an important aid to us in these difficult times. I look forward to meeting you when I return, and I shall tell you more of your uncle then. Until then, I shall keep you in my prayers.

Your Affectionate Aunt,
Augustine DuMaurier

There was something in the letter that puzzled Elisabet, and she carefully reread it. Yes, there it was: the phrase, "While I am away, Marie will teach you how to work in the bakery."

"What does my aunt want me to do in the bakery?" she asked Marie.

"Oh, do not worry. I will explain everything!" Marie replied confidently. "I will show you how to help Claude in the kitchen, how to arrange the shelves so the breads look beautiful, how to wait on customers and clear the tables. Soon, you will be a bakery assistant *par excellence*, like me!"

"There is some mistake!" Elisabet protested. "Certainly my aunt could not expect me to work in a bakery!"

Marie gave her an odd look. "Everyone must work, *non*? How else shall we eat?"

Elisabet sat down hard on a bale of cotton. How could she, who once had a household of servants, be expected to serve in a bakery like a common shop girl? It was unthinkable. For a moment, she considered running back to the ship. Perhaps she could convince the captain to take her back to Boston, back to . . .

And there she stopped. She had nothing to return to in Boston. No family, no house, no money. Papa was the only real family she had in the world, and she was closer to him here than in Boston. If she stayed here, perhaps there was some hope of finding Papa.

Marie tugged at her sleeve. "Come," she urged Elisabet. "It's getting late. We must return to the bakery before Claude worries, *non?*"

Elisabet picked up her satchel. Then she squared her shoulders and followed Marie across the levee. First, they passed by a meat market. The stalls were now closed, but dark clouds of flies and an overwhelming odor of rotting meat still hung in the air. "Gracious!" said Elisabet, putting her handkerchief to her nose. "This is even worse than the meat market in Boston!"

Marie grinned. "It *is* a bit strong in summer," she agreed. "But look, here is the Place d'Armes. Is it not beautiful?"

The two girls had crossed the street and entered a large grassy public square. "*Jolies fleurs!*" called out a boy who stood in front of a basket of orange, pink, and yellow blossoms. "Lovely flowers for lovely ladies!"

A strolling musician passed close to Elisabet and Marie. He played a lively tune on his violin, while a chattering monkey in a blue cap followed behind him, holding out a hat for coins. As soon as the monkey saw Marie, he scampered over eagerly.

Marie laughed. "*Bonsoir*, Pepe!" She pulled a broken roll from her pocket. "I saved this for you."

The monkey grabbed his treat from Marie and then looked expectantly at Elisabet. Elisabet was sorry to disappoint him. "I have nothing," she told the little monkey with a shrug of her shoulders.

The monkey shrugged his own tiny shoulders, then hurried back to the musician, who stopped his playing for a moment and walked over to the girls. "Wait a moment, Marie," he said in French. "I've heard that a ghost haunts your bakery. Can this be true?"

"*Non!*" Marie exclaimed, shaking her head. "Those stories are lies!"

"Perhaps, but perhaps not," said the musician, and he resumed his playing. As he walked away, his music seemed more mournful than before.

Elisabet was confused. She spoke French well, but the musician's accent had been hard for her to understand. "What did he mean?" she asked Marie. "What's this about a ghost?"

"Pay no attention," said Marie. "It is nothing but foolish rumors." She took Elisabet's elbow. "Come, we go this way."

Mystified, Elisabet followed the dark-haired girl down a diagonal path. They emerged on the other side of the park, near a magnificent church that towered above the square. Elisabet had to cover her eyes against the setting sun as she peered at the cross on top.

"What a lovely church!" she said. "What is it called?"

Marie looked at her as if she had just fallen out of the sky. "It is the Cathedral of Saint Louis, of course," she replied. "It is the finest cathedral in Louisiana. It is very famous."

Not in Boston, Elisabet thought, but she said nothing.

They walked by the cathedral and down a walkway covered by the overhanging roof of an imposing stucco and brick building. On their right, a soldier in a red and blue uniform stood at attention in front of a massive door. Elisabet wanted to ask what the building was, but she was afraid Marie would again be astonished by her ignorance.

Marie seemed to read her thoughts. "This is the Cabildo, where important government business is done. In 1803, the year I was born, the French signed the papers here selling all of the Louisiana Territory to the Americans."

"I was born that year, too," Elisabet said, almost to herself. "June sixth."

"Nobody knows what day I was born," Marie said matter-of-factly. "But the nuns at the orphanage baptized me the day the papers were signed, the twentieth of December. They named me Marie Jefferson, because Thomas Jefferson became our president that day." Marie paused at the corner. "This way," she directed.

The girls walked up a narrow road with shops and houses built right next to the street. Elisabet noticed that the shops had signs in French. She could understand the signs because she had grown up speaking French, first with her mother, then with a governess, and finally at school. Still, it seemed peculiar to be in a city where she had to translate the signs.

"Doesn't everyone in New Orleans speak English now?" she asked Marie. "After all, it is part of America."

"The Americans bought the land, *oui*," Marie agreed. "But they did not buy the people's hearts. Before this city was American, it was French. And before that, it was Spanish. And French again before that. So at heart, many people here are still Spanish or French."

"You speak English well."

Marie shrugged. "Monsieur DuMaurier taught me. He always spoke to me in English, and he taught me how to read and write a little, too. He said since we now belong to America, we should know its language."

Just then, the girls were passed by a backwoodsman wearing a coonskin cap and carrying a long rifle. Elisabet was struck by an odd odor as he walked past. Marie wrinkled her nose in distaste. "Personally, I do not mind Americans, except the ones who smell like bear grease. Ugh!"

The girls turned at the end of the block and headed down a street filled with houses painted pale pink, sky blue, and other pastel colors. The first-floor windows of these houses were arched like horseshoes and covered by bars or shutters. Windows on the upper floors opened onto balconies, which were enclosed by graceful wrought-iron fences.

Such odd-looking houses, Elisabet thought. *I hope my aunt and uncle's home doesn't look like these.*

All the houses were built next to the street. There were no tidy front gardens, like the one that grew in front of Elisabet's home in Boston. Instead, tropical blooms peeped out from window boxes on the balconies, and flowering vines entwined themselves around the iron grillwork.

"Don't the houses here have yards where children can play?" Elisabet inquired.

"They all have courtyards," said Marie. "Look—there's one." She pointed across the street, where a coachman had pulled up to a gate and opened it. Beyond the coach, Elisabet could see a walled courtyard, bordered by brightly blooming shrubs.

The two girls turned at the corner and walked down another street filled with small shops. They passed a dark young girl who was selling fruit. "Oranges!" she called out. "Juicy oranges!"

Elisabet looked at the orange-seller curiously. Once they were out of the girl's earshot, she asked Marie, "I see so many dark-skinned people here—are they all slaves? Is that girl a slave?"

Marie shrugged. "Perhaps. Most are slaves, but some are free. Take for example our baker, Claude. His father was a white man from France, and his mother was a woman of color from the Caribbean. He is a free man, and the best baker in all of New Orleans! People come from all over for his raisin *roulés*."

"Raisin *roulés?*" Elisabet repeated. "What are they?"

Marie smiled. "Sweet rolls made with cinnamon, honey, and raisins. Delicious!"

The mention of food made Elisabet realize she was very hungry. Her arms ached from carrying her satchel, too. "How much farther must we walk?" she asked.

"Not far," Marie said. "Do you need help carrying your bag?"

"No, thank you," Elisabet replied, even though the satchel seemed heavier with every step. "I am quite fine."

Marie led the way down a narrow side street. At an outdoor café halfway down the street, a group of fierce-looking men sat talking and drinking at a table. They wore the rough clothes of sailors, and one man, who looked taller and more powerful than the others, had a white scar running from the top of his nose to his ear.

Elisabet stared at the man in fascination. He wore a pistol in his belt and carried an enormous knife in a scabbard at his side. "Is that a pirate?" she whispered to Marie.

"Shhhhhh!" Marie hushed her. She quickly glanced at the men. "I do not know, but it is best not to stare at them."

The man, sensing Elisabet's eyes on him, looked up and glared at her. She quickly looked away and hurried on behind Marie. *Papa would know a pirate when he saw one,* she thought. *If only he were here!*

Marie interrupted her thoughts. "Here we are—just ahead," she said, pointing down a quiet side street. "Do you see the sign for the Horn of Plenty Bakery? It's the shape of a horn."

Elisabet saw a big wooden cornucopia hanging above a shop window halfway down the street. The painted cornucopia overflowed with carved wooden breads, rolls, and pastries. The sign signaled to all passersby, no matter what their language, that the bakery offered plenty of delicious foods.

"*That* is my uncle's bakery?" Elisabet asked.

She had hoped it would be like her father's favorite bakery in Boston—a big, thriving business with several counters and dozens of workers. This looked like a small, neighborhood shop, with only a few employees.

Marie, however, mistook Elisabet's disappointed surprise for amazement. "Yes, this is it!" she said, proudly pointing to the narrow three-story building. "You did not expect such a bakery, *non?*"

"No," Elisabet replied honestly. Looking in the Horn of Plenty's window, she saw only one long counter, with several shelves of baked goods behind it. Across from the counter, there were half a dozen tiny tables, each with two or three simple wooden chairs.

"Where is my aunt and uncle's house?" she asked.

"The DuMauriers' apartment is on the second floor." Marie pointed. "There, where you see the balcony with roses growing on it. You and I have the whole floor at the top."

Elisabet stopped in the street. "You mean their home is above the bakery?"

"But of course," said Marie impatiently. "Come, I will show you."

I have traveled over a thousand miles, Elisabet thought with dismay, *and now I must live above a little shop like this!*

A bell attached to the front door jangled merrily as Marie opened the door and gestured Elisabet inside. As soon as Elisabet walked in, she was met by a wave of warm, yeasty, sweet-smelling air. Suddenly, she felt overwhelmed by hunger.

"*Bienvenue!* Welcome!" a deep voice boomed from the back of the shop. A huge, bald, dark-skinned man came forward, wiping his hands on his apron.

Marie introduced Elisabet to Claude, and the big man gave her a kind smile. "We are glad you have arrived safely," he said in lilting, accented English. "You must be hungry. Come out to the kitchen."

The girls followed Claude through the shop. The first room held the counter as well as tables and chairs for customers. Next, there was a tiny hallway, with winding stairs leading to the second floor. Behind this hallway, a much smaller room contained shelves of coffee cups and plates and a tub for washing dishes.

They walked through this second room, out the back door, and down a few steps to a small courtyard enclosed by brick walls. The sky was growing dark, but Elisabet could see flowering vines growing around the edge of the courtyard, and a small garden in the center. To her right, outside stairs led up the main building to a small landing on the second floor. To her left was the bakery's kitchen, a narrow, single-story building with an open door and windows. Tempting smells filled the courtyard.

The girls followed Claude into the kitchen, where a gigantic oven took up the entire back wall. Looking around, Elisabet saw a fireplace with a kettle over it but no fire burning. Across from the fireplace were barrels of flour and sugar, shelves with other ingredients, and a waist-high wooden block for mixing and kneading dough. Above this block hung big wooden bowls, heavy rolling pins, huge wooden spoons, and other baking equipment. A small table flanked by two benches stood next to the open door.

Although all the equipment looked well worn, the kitchen was clean and tidy. A skinny boy of about fourteen was busy sweeping the floor.

Claude introduced him. "This is my assistant, Raoul. He is training to become a baker someday."

Raoul glanced up from his broom. "*Bonjour*," he said. "Your ship took so long to get here we wondered if you had been lost at sea."

"Raoul!" Marie protested.

Claude gave Raoul a stern look. Then he turned to Elisabet and gestured toward the small wooden table, which was neatly set with four pewter bowls and spoons. Two brightly burning candles in the middle of the table brought light to the darkening room. "Excuse his manners. Please, sit down and have some soup and bread."

Elisabet hesitated. How could she sit and eat a meal with these bakery workers? But the smell of fresh bread convinced her that she must either eat soon or faint from hunger. She put down her satchel and carefully sat at the very edge of the bench, as far away from the others as she could. Claude ladled out a rich, brown, onion-filled soup, which he topped with cheese. Then he passed around a long loaf of bread, and everyone tore off chunks.

As soon as Claude said the blessing, Elisabet took a bite of the bread. It was delicious—slightly crisp on the outside, warm and soft on the inside. She sampled the odd-looking soup. The beefy broth was hot and filling, and she quickly drained the bowl. After her second bowl of soup and three pieces of bread, Elisabet felt her strength returning. "This bread is wonderful," she told Claude. "I've never had anything quite like it."

"Really?" Claude seemed both pleased and surprised. "Do they not have good French bread in Boston?"

"Not like this. We do have delicious Boston brown bread—the best in the world, my father always says."

"Boston brown bread, eh? I have never heard of it." He paused, then added, "Madame DuMaurier told us of your father's imprisonment. We are all quite sorry. The British soldiers who captured him must be completely without honor to treat an American captain like that."

Elisabet nodded. Claude's kind words about her father warmed her heart just as the soup warmed her stomach. "Thank you," she said. "And I am sorry that my uncle died before I could meet him. He was my nearest relative after my father. I had looked forward to getting to know him."

Across the table, Raoul cleared his throat. Everyone looked at him. "Well," he said, "if the ghost appears again, perhaps you will still get a chance to meet your uncle."

Elisabet was so startled she dropped her spoon. It fell with a clang on her pewter bowl. "Pardon?" she asked. "What is all this about a ghost?"

CHAPTER 4

HAUNTED?

Claude scowled at his assistant. Raoul looked down at his soup.

"As I told you before, it is nothing," said Marie, with a dark glance at Raoul. "A few neighbors say that they have seen Monsieur DuMaurier's ghost since Madame left for Baton Rouge. They claim he haunts the empty apartment upstairs at night, carrying a candle. But that is impossible."

"Why is it impossible?" Raoul demanded. "Stranger things have happened. After all, we know that Monsieur left unfinished business here."

"What unfinished business?" Elisabet asked.

Claude ignored her question. He looked at Raoul sternly. "We will have no more talk of ghosts," he ordered. "You will frighten Monsieur's niece."

"I'm not frightened," Elisabet said, sitting up on the bench straighter than ever. But even as she spoke, she knew it was a lie. Suddenly, the soup seemed to have lost its flavor and the bread felt dry in her mouth. She pushed away her plate and looked outside at the growing darkness. Was it possible she would be sleeping tonight in a haunted house?

Claude seemed to read her thoughts. "You have no reason to be concerned, none at all. But if you girls would prefer not to be here alone tonight, Raoul will sleep in the shop."

"Oh, no!" Raoul protested. "I am tired of sleeping on the shop floor. I thought that once she came"—he jerked his head toward Elisabet—"I could sleep at home again."

"We do not need Raoul," Marie said scornfully. "We will be fine all alone, *non?*"

Marie looked at Elisabet for confirmation. Before Elisabet answered, she glanced outside again. In the darkness, the narrow bakery building loomed over the courtyard. *I don't want to sleep there*, Elisabet thought, *especially not alone!* But when Elisabet saw Marie waiting for her answer, her pride overcame her fear.

"Yes," she agreed without enthusiasm. "We will be fine."

"*Très bien*," said Claude, and he nodded with satisfaction. "Then Marie, you take Elisabet upstairs. Raoul and I will clean up here. Good night, girls. We will see you in the morning."

Marie took one of the candles from the table, and Elisabet picked up her satchel. She walked with Marie back across the courtyard to the bakery's outside stairs.

"Is that the way up?" she asked.

"*Non*," said Marie. "That leads only to your aunt's apartment on the second floor. We take the inside stairs to the top floor."

The two girls re-entered the empty bakery through the back door of the shop. Elisabet followed Marie into the hallway and up the narrow, winding staircase. The stairs creaked with each step they made, and Marie's flickering candle cast long shadows on the wall.

I wish I were anywhere but here, Elisabet thought as each step took her further into the dark building.

When they reached the second floor, Marie gestured to a closed door. "That is your aunt's apartment," she said. "Of course, now that Madame is gone, it is empty. Madame left instructions that no one should go in there while she is away."

"What about Claude and Raoul?" Elisabet asked as they climbed the next flight of stairs. "Where do they sleep?"

"Claude goes home to his family every night," Marie explained. "He and his wife have twin boys. When I was here by myself, Raoul slept downstairs in the shop. But now that you are here, he will go back to his mother's apartment. She lives on the next block. She is a widow with four other children. She depends on him for help, and he gives her everything he earns."

When the girls reached the third floor, they walked

down a short hallway with two doors opening onto it. "Here is the spare room," Marie announced, opening the door on the left.

Elisabet entered a hot, stuffy room, not much bigger than the playhouse her father had built her in Boston. But unlike her old playhouse—which had been charmingly decorated with miniature furniture—this room held only a narrow bed with a small table beside it and a washstand in the corner. The bed was encircled by gauze mosquito netting, but there were no curtains on the garret window, no pictures on the walls, no ornaments of any kind.

"It *is* spare, isn't it?" Elisabet murmured.

Marie opened the door on the right and showed Elisabet a larger room, with a bigger bed draped in mosquito netting and a wider window covered by a white curtain. This room was also very plain, but it included a wooden chair, a small chest of drawers covered by a white cloth, and a crucifix that hung above the bed.

"This is my room," Marie told Elisabet, looking as proud as if it were the finest mansion. "And now that you are here, we will share it."

Elisabet did not want to be alone at night. But she knew it would never do for the daughter of Captain John Holder to share a room with a shop assistant. "Thank you, but no," she told Marie. "I'll sleep in the spare room."

Marie looked startled. "Are you sure?" she asked. "There is plenty of room here for us both."

"Yes, I am sure."

For a moment, Marie looked hurt. Then she shrugged her shoulders. "As you wish," she said. She led Elisabet back to the smaller room. "We have only this one candle. You may use it tonight, but after that we must share it. *Bonne nuit.*"

"Good night," said Elisabet.

As soon as she was alone in the tiny closet of a room, Elisabet opened the window as far as she could. The damp night air carried mosquitoes, but it also brought a cooling breeze into the stifling hot room.

She changed into her night shift and hung her clothes over nails on the back of the door. Then she placed her family Bible on the small bedside table. She liked looking at it there. It was as if a small piece of home had traveled with her. Kneeling on the hard wooden floor, she said her prayers, ending with "Please watch over Papa and bring him back to me soon."

Finally, she arranged Agnes on the pillow and draped the mosquito netting carefully around the bed, leaving only one corner untucked so she could reach over and blow out the candle. When the candle was extinguished, the room was so black she could barely see Agnes. She felt for the doll and held her close.

"What am I going to do, Agnes?" she whispered. "Uncle Henri is dead. They want me to work in the bakery. And this building may be haunted!"

Elisabet lay in the dark, clutching Agnes and listening to every creak of the old building. What if the ghost should come in the night? What should she do? Her eyes were heavy with fatigue, but she was sure she would never be able to sleep.

⤳

The next thing Elisabet knew, someone was beside her bed. A hand was shaking her shoulder.

"Wake up!" Marie demanded. "Wake up!"

Bleary-eyed, Elisabet sat up in bed. "It's still dark outside!"

Marie laughed. "If we do not get up early, how will we be ready when people come to the bakery for their breakfasts? Claude and Raoul have already been at work for hours."

Still half asleep, Elisabet slowly got up and began to dress. Marie handed her a blue cotton work shift similar to her own. She said, "You may wear this. It will be cooler than your dress. The kitchen becomes very hot."

Elisabet eyed the dress. She might have to act like a shop assistant, but she refused to dress like one. "No, thank you," she told Marie firmly. "I will wear my own dress."

Marie shrugged, then hung the cotton dress on a nail next to Elisabet's dresses. "As you wish," she said. "It will be here for you if you change your mind. But now we must hurry."

A few minutes later, Elisabet was following Marie out the back door of the shop, across the courtyard, and into the kitchen. A fire blazed in the big oven and filled the kitchen with waves of heat. *No wonder they keep the oven out here in the courtyard*, Elisabet thought. *If it were inside, the shop would be so hot no one would come in.*

The little table was set by the open door at the cooler end of the kitchen. Elisabet sat down at the far end of the bench she shared with Marie. She sipped *café au lait*, coffee mixed with hot milk. Then Claude brought out a plateful of *beignets*, fried pastries that were crispy and sweet on the outside, light and soft on the inside. The first *beignet* Elisabet tried was so good, she decided to have a second.

"That was wonderful," Elisabet exclaimed as she ate the last morsel of the second pastry. "Now I must go to the levee. I want to ask the ship captains if they have word of the *Sophie*."

Claude and Marie exchanged looks. Then Claude said, "I am afraid that will not be possible. It would be quite unsafe for a girl like you, a girl who knows nothing of New Orleans, to walk around alone on the levee."

"But my father may be very near," Elisabet protested. "I must get news of him."

"Many people come to the bakery, and we get all the news right here. If your father's ship is sighted, we will hear of it. You must not go wandering about by yourself. Do you understand?"

Elisabet thought for a moment. She did *understand*, but that did not mean she planned to obey. She nodded her head.

"Good," Claude smiled. "You are needed here at the bakery. With Madame DuMaurier gone, we are especially short-handed. Now we must all get to work. Our first customers will arrive any moment."

Just then, the bell attached to the front door jangled. Marie got up abruptly. "Come," she told Elisabet, "I will show you how to help in the shop. There is a lot to learn."

Following Marie out of the kitchen and across the courtyard, Elisabet thought the little shop assistant was trying to make herself sound important. After all, how difficult could it be to sell someone a roll or pastry?

But Elisabet soon discovered there was more to bakery work than handing a customer his bread and collecting his money. First, Marie explained, she had to smile and be pleasant to the customers. "We need their business," Marie emphasized. "As Madame always says, if people do not buy bread from us, we ourselves will have no bread to eat."

Elisabet listened to Marie, but decided privately that she would be pleasant only to people who looked educated and well-bred. She would serve the other, rougher customers if she must. She would even be polite to them. But smile and say *bonjour*? Never.

Marie explained that in addition to selling, the two girls were responsible for making sure the shelves were always filled with fresh-baked breads, telling Claude what items were in short supply, making and serving coffee, cleaning the tables, and washing the dishes in the back room.

Just after sunrise, more customers began to arrive. A few of these early customers chose to sit at the little tables and sip coffee with their pastries. Most, however, simply picked out their fresh bread and pastries and took their purchases with them.

I can do this easily, thought Elisabet as she served her third customer.

Soon, however, the customers started coming more quickly. People arrived in groups of two or three, and the tables began to fill. One man ordered eight different items, and Elisabet had to figure the prices quickly in her head and then work out the change. Meanwhile, customers at the tables called out, "Girl, more coffee!" The shelves started to empty, but Elisabet was too busy waiting on customers to refill them.

The lines at the counter grew longer, and the customers grew more impatient. "You gave me the wrong change!" an angry workman accused her. "You owe me five cents!"

"Don't you have more of those raisin *roulés*?" a mother with three young children complained. "We walked all this way for your raisin *roulés*."

"Coffee, girl!" a loud man at a table demanded.

Elisabet felt close to tears. But Marie, who had been busy in the kitchen, came to the rescue. "Here is your money, *monsieur*. We are sorry for the mistake," she told the angry man who was waiting for his change. "And *madame*, your raisin *roulés* will be ready in just one moment. Please, have some coffee while you wait."

Then Marie whispered to Elisabet, "You serve the coffee, then go ask Claude for more raisin *roulés*. I will tend the counter."

With great relief, Elisabet left the counter and poured coffee for the customers waiting at the tables. *Perhaps this will be harder than I expected*, she thought.

Indeed, for the next hour, Elisabet was always hurrying and always arriving late. Then the rush ended as suddenly as it had begun. The bakery emptied out. There was no one in line, and only a few people were left at the tables.

"That was dreadful!" Elisabet exclaimed when she and Marie were alone behind the counter. "Are the mornings always like that?"

"*Oui*," Marie shrugged. "But it will become easier as you get used to it."

I don't ever want to get used to it, Elisabet thought. *I want to find my father and go back to Boston.* But she said nothing.

"I am going back to help Claude," Marie continued. "Call me if you need me."

Customers trickled in slowly now, and Elisabet had

more time to study them. She paid special attention when a pretty, plump blond girl about her own age came into the bakery with her father, a distinguished-looking gentleman who carried a gold-tipped cane.

"Well, Caroline," the father asked in a Yankee accent. "What will you have today?"

"The lemon one, Papa," the daughter said, pointing to a rich pastry filled with lemon custard. "It will match my new gown," she giggled, gesturing at her fashionably cut lemon-colored silk dress.

I once had dresses as fine as that, Elisabet thought. *I would love to have a dress just that color—perhaps trimmed with a bit of lace . . .*

The man interrupted her daydreams. "We'll take two of those," he told Elisabet, motioning to the pastries with his cane. He handed Elisabet a gold coin and she quickly made change. She decided that both the father and daughter looked educated and well-bred. In fact, they looked like the sort of people she might have been friends with in Boston. She favored them with a smile and a pleasant "Thank you." But they did not even look at her.

"We must hurry, Papa," the daughter said, drawing her white-gloved hand through her father's arm. "Mademoiselle will be ever so cross if I'm late for my French lesson."

As Elisabet watched the father and daughter leave the store and walk down the street, talking and laughing, she felt a pain as if someone had stabbed her in the ribs. She remembered that not so long ago, *her father* had taken *her* out for special treats. Now her father was gone, and she was forced to work behind the counter in a bakery.

I will find Papa, she resolved to herself, *and I'll leave here as soon as I can.*

Yet as the morning wore on, Elisabet could find no opportunity for escape. Instead, Marie insisted on trying to teach her all about the bakery.

"These are the flute loaves," she said, pointing to long, skinny loaves of bread. "And over there are the *pistolettes.*"

"Little pistols?" Elisabet echoed in surprise, looking about for a pair of pistols. "What do you mean?"

Marie laughed. "Not pistols that you shoot—these are *pistolettes* that you eat." She gestured at a basket of crusty rolls. "They're called *pistolettes* because they say gentlemen eat them for breakfast before a duel. Other customers like them, too. Here, why don't you put this basket out?"

Elisabet dumped the fresh batch of *pistolettes* onto the bakery shelf, then turned to walk away.

"*Non!* Not like that," Marie said. "We must arrange them in neat rows." She pointed to the other shelves above the counter. "See how the pastries are lined up just so? Do they not look attractive that way?"

"People buy the rolls to eat, not to look at," said Elisabet in exasperation. "It doesn't matter how they are arranged!"

Marie gave her a horrified look. "Of course it matters!"

she said. She began to rearrange the *pistolettes* expertly. "As Madame always says, 'We eat with our eyes as well as our stomachs.' If everything looks delicious, people will buy more. Watch how I fix this shelf."

But as soon as Marie turned her attention to the rolls, Elisabet began staring out the window. Outside, carriages and heavy work wagons rolled noisily down the center of the street. Workmen were in the street too, pushing heavy wheelbarrows of merchandise. On both *banquettes*, as Marie called the raised wooden sidewalks, streams of people walked by. Elisabet could see couples strolling arm in arm, women chatting as they carried their baskets to market, ragged children playing and shouting, and businessmen in dark coats talking seriously as they walked.

Several rough-looking sailors passed by, and Elisabet studied them closely. *Maybe those men are pirates*, Elisabet wondered. *Or maybe they're privateers. I wonder if pirates really feed children to the sharks or—*

"*Elisabet!*" Marie broke into her thoughts. "How can I show you anything if you keep looking outside?"

Elisabet's cheeks flushed. How dare this girl treat her as if she were a dunce at school! "Why shouldn't I look outside?" she defended herself. "It's more interesting outside than it is in here!"

"Fine!" Marie grabbed a tray and headed back to the kitchen. "Since you already know everything about arranging the shelves, I will go get more pastries."

Left on her own in the empty bakery, Elisabet tossed back her head and once again started watching the people outside.

One man in particular caught Elisabet's attention. He was tall and heavyset, with a drooping black mustache and a nose that looked as if it had been chewed off. Elisabet studied the man as he stopped in front of the Horn of Plenty and seemed to examine the bakery's sign.

I hope he doesn't come in here, Elisabet thought. *I don't like the way he looks.*

The man spent a long time outside the bakery. Finally, he seemed to make up his mind. He strode through the door just as Marie was returning to the counter with a tray full of pastries. Marie smiled at him. "May I help you, *monsieur?*"

"I must see Madame DuMaurier," the man barked.

"I am sorry, *monsieur*, but Madame DuMaurier is away," Marie replied politely.

The man's eyes narrowed. "Are you lying to me, girl?" he asked in a threatening tone.

Elisabet was shocked by the man's rudeness. "Of course she's not lying," she told the man. "My aunt is in Baton Rouge."

The man turned to Elisabet. "Aunt, eh? So Madame DuMaurier is your aunt?"

The man's squinting gray eyes looked hard into Elisabet's own. She nodded, too scared to speak. With one hand, he grabbed her chin, bringing her face so close to his that she smelled his foul breath.

"Well, missy, you tell your aunt that Lucas McCain just got back in town," the man rasped. "DuMaurier owed me money. I've heard about that treasure map he hid away, and I've come to collect it. That map should be mine, you understand?"

Elisabet tried to nod again. McCain held her chin so tightly she could barely move. Marie grabbed at McCain's arm and tried to loosen his grip. "You leave her alone," Marie yelled at him. "Get out of here!"

McCain used his free hand to push Marie away. Then he turned again to Elisabet. Still holding her by the chin, he pulled her even closer. "You tell your aunt that if she don't give me the map, she'll be sorry," McCain threatened. With one dirty fingernail, he cut an imaginary line across her throat, as if he were planning to slit it with a knife. "You'll *all* be sorry!"

CHAPTER 5
THE MISSING MAP

Claude, who had heard the uproar, suddenly emerged from the back of the bakery carrying a heavy wooden rolling pin in one hand.

"Eh! What's going on here?" he demanded. "What do you think you are doing?"

McCain took one look at Claude's towering frame and released Elisabet. "Nothing that concerns a cook," he snarled.

"Everything here concerns me," said Claude. He stepped closer to McCain, holding the big rolling pin like a club. "Now get out!"

"Pah!" McCain spat in disgust. "I don't have time for cooks." He looked menacingly at Elisabet. "Just remember what I said!" Then he stalked out of the bakery door, slamming it after himself.

Elisabet felt weak with relief as she saw McCain head down the street. "What was he talking about?" she asked

Marie breathlessly. "What treasure map?"

Claude and Marie looked at each other, and Elisabet guessed they were deciding how much they should tell her. At last Claude said, "Perhaps you should know that long before Monsieur DuMaurier was a baker, he was a smuggler."

"My uncle—a smuggler!" Elisabet exclaimed. "Isn't that someone who brings things into the country illegally? Don't they hang people for that?"

"Sometimes," Claude admitted. "But there are many ways in and out of this city the government doesn't know about. And if they tried to hang all the smugglers in New Orleans, they would soon run out of rope."

"I see," Elisabet said. Yet in her heart she didn't understand at all. How could her uncle have been an outlaw? "Are you *sure* he was a smuggler?"

Claude smiled. "*Oui*, he was the greatest smuggler of his time. They called him the Bayou Fox because he knew every inch of the bayous around here. People say he had a hundred different routes through the swamps. Many times the authorities tried to catch him, and they never succeeded. He became rich. Very, very rich."

"What happened?" Elisabet asked, her curiosity overcoming her horror at being related to a criminal.

"One day, about seven years ago, Monsieur Henri became so sick he was close to death," Claude said. "When he recovered, he gave up smuggling, freed the slaves he owned, and gave his riches to the church. At first, many people thought the Bayou Fox was playing another trick. But *non*, he had changed completely. He married Madame Augustine, a widow who owned this bakery. They lived happily together until Monsieur died suddenly this summer."

For a moment, the bakery was silent. Then Elisabet asked, "But that man said there was a treasure map. What did he mean?"

"The day Monsieur Henri died, he and Marie were working together in the shop," Claude continued. "It was very busy. Monsieur was serving customers, when suddenly he grabbed his chest. He cried out, 'My heart!' and fell to the floor. Before he died, he said something about a map. Marie was closest to him."

"People were crowding around Monsieur, and he pointed up, like this," said Marie, making a gesture toward the ceiling. "Then he said to me in English, 'My map—I saved it. Very important . . . must not get into . . . wrong hands. Look in the night . . . up . . .' He tried to say more, but I could not understand it."

Marie's voice broke. "Then he was gone."

"After the funeral, we looked everywhere for the map—during the day and the night," Claude said.

"We looked upstairs and down, we looked in every drawer, through all of Monsieur's papers, under every piece of furniture," Marie added. "Madame DuMaurier even offered to give half of whatever the map is worth to whichever of us could find it. But so far, no one has had any luck."

Elisabet thought back to Lucas McCain's threats. "Is it really a treasure map?"

Marie shrugged. "We do not know. But the shop was crowded that day, and some of the customers overheard Monsieur's last words. As soon as people heard that the Bayou Fox spoke of a map as he lay dying—well, naturally they assumed it was a map to some hidden treasure."

"Of course, it could be another kind of map," Claude cautioned. "Perhaps he left a guide to the swamps and bayous. That too would be valuable."

"Why would a map of the swamps be valuable?" Elisabet asked, more mystified than ever.

"There are many who would love to have such a map— smugglers, pirates, even the British if they are planning to attack New Orleans," explained Claude. "Still, people like Monsieur McCain are convinced the map leads to a greater treasure. They think the Bayou Fox did not give all his riches to the church. They believe he buried treasure in the swamps somewhere."

"Treasure!" said an excited voice. It was Raoul, who had come in from the kitchen all covered in flour. "Has the treasure map been found?"

Claude clapped his hand on Raoul's shoulder. "*Non*, my boy, not yet. Come, we must all get back to work." He started toward the kitchen. Then he paused and turned back to Elisabet and Marie. "I do not think we will see Monsieur McCain again. But if he should come back, let me know immediately. I do not want him causing more trouble."

After Claude left, Elisabet turned to Marie. Swallowing her pride, she told the shop assistant, "You were very brave to fight that man. Thank you for coming to my aid."

"It was nothing," Marie shrugged. "That Monsieur McCain is a coward and a bully. The great Bayou Fox never would have had dealings with such a snake—much less owed him money. Monsieur McCain was only trying to scare us so we would tell him where the map is."

"Well, he scared me," Elisabet admitted. She rubbed her chin, which was still sore from the man's vicious grip.

The bell on the door jangled as two customers walked in. Soon both girls were back to work. Marie waited on the customers while Elisabet wiped the tables and put out clean dishes.

As she worked, Elisabet's thoughts returned to Lucas McCain, and she remembered how his cold gray eyes stared at her. *Did Uncle Henri's missing map really lead to treasure?* she wondered.

She wished she had time to think about the mysterious map, but customers began pouring into the bakery to buy bread for their midday meals. As soon as the rush ended, Claude said he was going home to his family for dinner.

"Your meal is in the kitchen," he told the girls. "I'll be back in a few hours." He closed the curtains over the front window and locked the front door behind him.

"Are we done for the day?" Elisabet asked hopefully.

Marie laughed. "It is only midday. But we must eat, *non*? We will go back to work after our siesta."

Elisabet did not know what a siesta was, but she suddenly realized she was hungry. Even though she had been surrounded by food all morning, she had eaten nothing since her *beignets* before dawn. She followed Marie back to the kitchen, where Claude had left them a spicy shrimp-and-okra gumbo served with rice, bread, and pastries for dessert.

After their midday dinner, Raoul announced he would take his siesta in the shop. "I'm too tired to go home," he said with a yawn, pulling out an empty flour sack to lie on. "I'll just sleep here."

The big meal, combined with the sweltering afternoon heat, had left Elisabet yawning, too. She and Marie climbed the stairs to the top floor. "Does everyone here nap in the middle of the day?" Elisabet asked.

"Why work when it is hottest?" Marie replied.

For Elisabet, the siesta was all too short. It seemed she had just put her arms around Agnes and closed her eyes, when Marie was shaking her shoulder and telling her it was time to return to work.

The late afternoon in the bakery was much like the

morning. There were busy periods, when dozens of customers would suddenly arrive and Elisabet and Marie would have to run to serve everyone. Then there were quiet times, when the bakery was almost deserted.

During the quiet times, Elisabet found herself again staring out the window, but now her curiosity was mixed with dread. Every time she looked at the street, she wondered if Lucas McCain might be there. Once she caught sight of a man who looked like McCain. He was across the street, however, and she could not get a good view of him before a carriage passed in front of the bakery. By the time the carriage was gone, so was the man.

"Marie," she whispered to the other girl. "I think I just saw Lucas McCain again. I think he's out there."

Marie peered out the window and shook her head. "I do not see him anywhere," she said. "Do not worry yourself. He will probably never come again. If he does, Claude will take care of him."

Elisabet was not convinced. She wanted to ask Marie how she could be so sure, but a sailor at a nearby table held up his empty coffee cup.

"Coffee!" the sailor demanded. "Another coffee, girl!"

Elisabet was forced to return to her work. But she had seen the determination in McCain's cold eyes, and she was sure he would try again to get the treasure map. For the rest of the afternoon, she kept watch on the street outside.

A gang of slaves bound by chains passed the bakery.

One of the slaves was a skinny boy about Elisabet's age, who paused for a moment and looked longingly at the breads. A big white man smacked the boy and ordered him to hurry up.

Elisabet shuddered as she watched the boy stumble up the street. *It's bad enough to work in this steaming bakery,* she thought. *I can't imagine how awful it must be to be a slave.*

When the sun set, Claude once again closed the curtains and locked the doors. After the bakery was cleaned and swept, they all sat down to a meal of soup and bread. Elisabet was so tired she could barely eat, but she worried about the long night ahead. Marie had told her there was no extra candle for the spare room. How could she possibly go to bed in darkness tonight?

As the two girls climbed the stairs together that night, Marie held the candle. Its flickering light illuminated the dark hall enough for Elisabet to find her door. On opening the door, she saw that her window allowed just enough moonlight for her to dimly see the room.

"Good night," she said to Marie.

"*Bonne nuit,*" Marie replied crisply, and closed her door.

Elisabet quickly changed into her night shift. Soon she was lying in bed under the mosquito netting with Agnes in her arms. She closed her eyes and smelled the sweet, slightly musty smell of Agnes's dress, and for a moment, she imagined herself back in Boston. She remembered all the evenings when Papa had read her bedtime stories.

After the stories, he always tucked Elisabet and her doll together into Elisabet's beautiful mahogany bed with its soft feather mattress and crisp linen sheets.

And then he always gave her a kiss on each cheek. "One kiss is from your mama in heaven," he would say. "And one is from me. Good night, my precious Elisa."

I would give anything in the world, Elisabet thought, *if Papa and I could be back in Boston again.*

Her mind went back to all the strange events of the day—Lucas McCain, his threats, and the mystery of the missing map. She remembered how Marie had said that whoever found the map could keep half the treasure. *If I could find the map, maybe I could use the treasure to ransom Papa*, she thought excitedly. *But how can I find it?*

Elisabet fell asleep with questions whirling in her head. Suddenly, she awoke with a start. For a moment, she didn't know where she was. Then everything came back to her—Lucas McCain, the bakery, the ghost. She realized she had been awakened by a noise.

THUD! There it was again! It sounded as if it were coming from the apartment downstairs. Elisabet clutched Agnes tightly. *Could it be the ghost?* she wondered. *Was it walking downstairs even now? Would it come upstairs?*

Even though the room was hot, Elisabet felt goose bumps of fear. Heart pounding, she lay awake in the dark and listened for more noises. At first, there were several more thuds. Then she heard only the creaking of the house.

The tiny room became eerily silent, and Elisabet began to wish she had accepted Marie's offer to share her room.

It seemed like hours before she fell asleep again. In the morning, she asked Marie, "Did you hear noises last night?"

"*Non*," Marie said cautiously. "Did you?"

"Yes! It sounded as if someone was downstairs."

"Tell Claude," Marie urged.

Over breakfast, Elisabet told Claude about the loud thuds in the night. He checked the outside doors and windows and found all of them locked as he had left them the night before. "It might have been rats," he suggested. "Sometimes we get big ones—I suppose they smell the food here. I'll borrow the neighbor's cat and see if it catches anything."

"It didn't sound like a rat," Elisabet insisted. "It sounded more like a person or a . . ." She paused.

"A ghost?" Raoul teased. "Maybe it was a ghost rat!"

Elisabet bit her lip. She knew she had heard something. But what was it?

CHAPTER 6
A CAPTAIN'S RANSOM

Elisabet soon found herself settling into a routine at the Horn of Plenty. Every day except Sunday, when the bakery was closed, she and Marie began work before dawn. They took a break at midday for their dinner and a too-short siesta. Then they went back to work again until Claude locked the doors in the early evening.

The work was hard, and the bakery was hotter than Elisabet had ever believed possible. At first, she insisted on wearing the clothes she had brought from Boston: long-sleeved, heavy linen dresses, stockings, and shoes. But the clothes that had looked so proper and respectable in Boston proved to be almost unbearable in the sweltering New Orleans bakery.

One morning, she awoke to discover that the day was already oppressively hot—and the sun had not even risen yet. In desperation, she decided to try on the short-sleeved blue cotton work shift Marie had given her. She put on the light dress, tied a white apron over it, and walked barefoot, just like Marie. She was amazed to find how much cooler she felt.

When she walked into the kitchen wearing the work shift, Claude and Marie smiled but tactfully said nothing. Raoul laughed out loud. "We all wondered how much longer you were going to wear those heavy things. You are one of us now, eh?"

One of us! Raoul's words came as a shock to Elisabet. *I will never become just another shop assistant*, she resolved to herself. *I will get back to Boston.*

But how? Every day, she tried to gain information about her father. Whenever she waited on customers, she listened to their conversations in hope of picking up some scrap of news about the British ship *Sophie* or even a rumor about prisoners of war. She paid special attention to the sailors, but all they ever seemed to do was brag about their last voyage or complain about the weather.

On the eighth day, however, Elisabet's eavesdropping proved useful. She was pouring coffee for an elderly lady when she overheard a conversation between two businessmen at the next table.

"I received some news about Jean Lafitte this morning," the taller of the two told his companion. He had bushy eyebrows and a long mustache that waggled as he spoke. He brushed it carefully with his napkin. "He may be making a deal with the British navy."

The words "British navy" caught Elisabet's attention. She slowly began to gather the dirty coffee cups at the next table.

"Ha!" the other businessman snorted. He was a stocky, bald man who was trying to stuff a pastry into his mouth. When he finally swallowed, he said, "Lafitte would never deal with those dirty Brits. Why should he? He's got everything he wants right here in New Orleans."

The man with bushy eyebrows took a long, slow sip of coffee. "If Lafitte isn't allying himself with the British, why is their ship, the *Sophie*, anchored off his base in Barataria?"

The *Sophie*! Elisabet was so startled she knocked a coffee cup off the table. It fell to the floor with a crash, and the businessmen looked up in surprise. Elisabet mumbled an apology and, grabbing the broken pieces, hurried back to the kitchen.

"Claude!" she said excitedly. "I finally have news of my father!"

She quickly told the big baker what she had overheard. Then she asked, "Where is Barataria? If the ship holding Papa is anchored there, I must go there too!"

Raoul, who had been listening in on the conversation, hooted with laughter. "Nobody in their right mind would *want* to go to Barataria. Lafitte's got more than a thousand pirates down there—and any one of 'em would as soon knife you in the back as look at you."

Elisabet swallowed hard. She looked over at Claude, who was rolling out a large sheet of pastry dough. He shrugged. "It is not a community you would want to visit. Besides, it is some distance away. Look here . . ."

Claude took an orange and put it in the center of the dough. "Imagine this orange is New Orleans, and here"—he took a knife and drew a long wavy line to the south and east of the orange—"is the Mississippi River. Well, Lafitte's Barataria is all the way down here." He put a walnut near the edge of the dough circle, west of the Mississippi River. "It's on Grande Terre Island, where Barataria Bay meets the Gulf of Mexico."

"How long would it take to get there?" Elisabet asked, looking with dismay at the distant walnut.

"Well," Claude answered, "people say Lafitte knows the swamps so well he can travel here from Barataria in twenty-four hours. They say he comes here at night, even though there is a warrant out for his arrest. But for anyone else . . ." Claude paused. "It would be at least a two-day trip, probably more—even supposing you could find someone who was willing to take you there, which is very unlikely."

"And what would you do if you got there?" Raoul teased. "Row out to the boat and attack the British by yourself?"

Elisabet tried to ignore Raoul, but she knew he was

right. Yet to have her father so near and be unable to see him! It was almost more than she could bear.

"There must be something I can do!" she said.

Claude thought for a moment as he continued to roll out the dough. "If you had a lawyer and a lot of money, you could try to ransom your father, but since you do not have either—"

"Wait," Elisabet cried. "I do know a lawyer. I met him on the boat. He was very nice, and he gave me his card. He said I could call on him if I ever needed help. His name is Mr. Robinson."

"I know of Monsieur Robinson," announced Marie as she hurried into the kitchen with a tray to refill. "He is one of the lawyers working to free Jean Lafitte's brother, Pierre, from jail."

"That is true," said Claude. "Pierre Lafitte is in prison for smuggling. The government would like to imprison Jean Lafitte too, if only they could catch him. Monsieur Robinson is one of the Lafitte brothers' lawyers."

"But how can pirates hire a lawyer?" Elisabet asked.

Claude laughed. "Jean Lafitte is so rich he can hire almost anyone. Your friend Monsieur Robinson sometimes comes to the bakery. The next time he comes, you can tell him about your father. Perhaps he could give you some advice."

"But I can't wait," Elisabet protested. "I must go see him now."

"You have no money to hire a lawyer," Claude reminded her gently. He picked up his peel, a long-handled flat wooden shovel he used to reach into the huge oven. He removed golden brown loaves of bread from the oven and placed them on Marie's empty tray. "And besides, we need you in the bakery."

"*Oui*," Marie agreed. "The customers are beginning to line up now. And we must bring out more breads. Come, Elisabet, they are waiting for us."

Reluctantly, Elisabet returned to the front shop. All through the morning she thought about how she could find her father. By the time Claude closed the shop for their afternoon meal, she had made up her mind. She must see Mr. Robinson today—whether Claude approved or not.

Elisabet waited until after they had cleared the dishes and she and Marie had gone up to their rooms for their afternoon siesta. She left the door to her room open a crack and listened. Finally, the sound of soft snoring in the next room signaled that Marie had gone to sleep.

Very quietly, Elisabet took off her work shift and pulled stockings over her dusty bare feet. She changed into her good gray linen dress, tied her best bonnet over her hair, and slipped Mr. Robinson's card into her pocket. Then she tiptoed down the stairs, carrying her shoes in one hand.

Remembering the bell attached to the front door, she

crept through the shop, where Raoul was sleeping on his flour sack. She was almost at the door when Raoul stirred in his sleep. Elisabet froze. What excuse could she give if he awoke and found her sneaking out?

She held her breath while Raoul muttered something and then rolled over again. She waited until he seemed to be sleeping soundly, and then she let herself out the back door, easing it closed behind her. When she was finally on the street, she took a deep breath and looked around. There was no sign of anyone she knew. She was free.

Now where should she go? Sometimes she and Marie had taken short walks together before bed. But she had never explored New Orleans on her own. In fact, she realized, she had never before gone far in any city by herself. In Boston, there had always been someone—Papa, Mrs. Rigsby, a governess—to go with her. Here she was on her own.

She looked down at the card in her hand. It read:

Jeremiah Robinson, Esq.
Attorney-at-law
Seven Rue du Chevalier
New Orleans

She had no idea where the Rue du Chevalier might be. She decided to walk south toward the Saint Louis Cathedral because its bell towers made it an easy landmark to find. As she walked, she checked all the streets she passed.

There was no sign of the Rue du Chevalier. Most of the city's residents had gone home to rest in the midday heat, and the steaming streets were quiet, almost deserted, except for dogs that lay panting in the shade of the buildings. Even the bright yellow and orange flowers in the window boxes look tired and wilted in the heat.

Elisabet looked for someone who could help her find her way, but most of the people she saw were tough-looking men. She remembered Mrs. Murdoch's warnings about pirates and pickpockets, and she hurried past these men. Finally, she asked a ragged boy if he knew where the Rue du Chevalier was. He said he didn't know, but did she have any food?

Elisabet nodded. Marie had taught her always to carry stale rolls in her pocket in case she came across a hungry child or animal. She gave the boy a roll and he thanked her.

"Try that way," the boy suggested, pointing west. "Seems I might have heard of a street like that over there."

Not feeling very hopeful, Elisabet trudged west. Her face was dripping sweat, and she began to wonder if she would ever find the Rue du Chevalier. She was in a poor part of town now, and the streets smelled of garbage. Beggars sat in the shade of doorways.

"Hey, girl!" a one-legged man cried out in French. "You got money for an old cripple?"

Elisabet shook her head and walked on quickly, carefully avoiding the eyes of other beggars. Three blocks later, she was in a neighborhood of small shops and businesses. A dark-skinned girl about her own age was selling baskets on the sidewalk. "*Pardon*, would you know where the Rue du Chevalier is?" Elisabet asked in French.

"*Oui*," the girl replied. "It's a very small street, about five blocks from here. Look, you go down one block here, then turn left and go four blocks more. There are beautiful homes there. You will know you have reached the Rue du Chevalier because on the corner there is a big statue of a man riding a horse. The man who owns that house was a great general once, and the statue was made to look just like him."

"*Merci!*" Elisabet exclaimed. Hurrying on, she was surprised to discover that the street she was looking for was only a few blocks from the Horn of Plenty—but in the opposite direction from where she had first walked.

A life-size statue of a man on horseback marked the corner of the Rue du Chevalier, just as the girl had described it. Number seven was four houses from the corner. It was a two-story brick and stucco house with white shutters on the windows and a wide wood front door. A long balcony with a delicate wrought-iron railing stretched the width of the second floor, and pink, red, and yellow flowers brought color to boxes in front of every window.

Walking up to the house's heavy, intricately carved front door, Elisabet hesitated. *What if he doesn't remember me?* she thought. *Or what if he refuses to see me?*

She fingered Mr. Robinson's card. *He told me to call on him if I ever needed help*, she reminded herself. *And I have never needed help more than I do right now.*

Elisabet picked up the big brass door knocker and let it fall. Immediately, she heard a deep baying beyond the door. *Aroooo! Arooo! Arooooooooo!*

"Hush, Brutus! Hush, Caesar!" came a woman's voice. "I hear it! Now sit and stay!" In a moment, a tall, gray-haired woman wearing a starched apron opened the door just a crack. She peered down at Elisabet. "Good afternoon," she said, sounding surprised to see a young girl on the doorstep. "May I help you?"

"Good—good afternoon, ma'am," Elisabet stammered. "I'd like to see Mr. Robinson, please."

"Mr. Robinson is busy, child," the woman said firmly. "Would you care to leave a message?"

"No, ma'am," Elisabet blurted out. "I . . . I can't leave. I really must see him. My name is Elisabet Holder, and I met him on the boat. He said I should call on him if I ever needed help."

"I see," the woman said, but it was clear from her voice that she did not see at all. She paused, looked at Elisabet closely, then seemed to make up her mind. "Come inside, and you can wait until Mr. Robinson's meeting is over. He should be finished in an hour or so."

"Thank you, ma'am," Elisabet said. The woman ushered

Elisabet inside the door, where she was met by two of the biggest dogs she had ever seen. They had broad chests and short black fur with patches of brown. Their heads were level with Elisabet's chest, and they sniffed her curiously. Then they wagged their tails. Elisabet patted their heads, and they thumped their tails even harder.

"These are Brutus and Caesar," said the woman, gesturing to the big dogs. "They're Mr. Robinson's pets. They like children, girls in particular, so you should not have any problem with them. Come this way."

The housekeeper led Elisabet down the hallway. They passed closed doors, which she assumed led to a parlor. Then the housekeeper opened double doors that led into a small study lined with books on every wall. An enormous mahogany desk took up most of the room. A matching mahogany chair was placed behind the desk, and two smaller chairs sat across from it.

"You may sit there," the woman said, indicating one of the smaller chairs. "When Mr. Robinson is finished with his meeting, I shall let him know you are here."

As soon as Elisabet sat down, both dogs sat by her feet and tried to nose their heads onto her lap. Brutus started sniffing her pocket.

Elisabet laughed. "You smell my other roll, don't you, boy? Here you are." She took the roll and divided it, giving half to each of the dogs. They gobbled up the crumbs and thumped their tails. Then Elisabet patted their heads and scratched behind their ears. And she waited. And waited.

Sometimes she could hear voices from the parlor, but mostly all she could hear was the ticking of the large clock on the mantelpiece. An hour passed, and Elisabet knew that by now she would be missed at the bakery. What would Claude and Marie think? Would they believe she had run away? She wished she had left a note telling them not to worry. But it was too late now.

Another hour passed. Elisabet walked around the room. The comforting smells of old, leather-bound books and furniture polished with beeswax reminded her of Papa's study back in Boston. She had loved to look at Papa's books, especially the illustrated *Pilgrim's Progress*. But most of the books on Mr. Robinson's shelves were written in Latin and had no pictures. So Elisabet passed the time by patting the dogs.

When the mantel clock chimed another half hour, Elisabet began to despair. "Where *is* Mr. Robinson?" she asked the dogs. "Is he even here?"

Suddenly, both dogs bounded to the door, tails wagging. The study door opened, and Mr. Robinson strode in, dressed in a formal black suit. "Well, if it isn't my young friend from the *Marissa*! Hello, Elisabet!" He shook her hand warmly, then sat down in his chair. "I apologize for having kept you waiting. My housekeeper just told me you were here. How are you?"

"I am well, sir," Elisabet said. "And I have news of my

father!" She quickly outlined what she had heard about the *Sophie*. "I must discover whether my father is aboard that ship, and if he is, find some way to free him. You will help me, won't you?"

Mr. Robinson leaned back in his chair and shook his head. "I'm sorry, but I don't know what I could do. Even if we should be fortunate enough to find your father on the *Sophie*, the only way the British would free him is if you paid a ransom."

"How much would such a ransom be?"

"Well," the lawyer said, "I'd guess about two thousand dollars, perhaps more."

"Two thousand dollars!" Elisabet echoed. Her heart fell. Claude had warned she would need money to buy her father's freedom, but she had never imagined it would be such a huge sum.

"Is there any way you could raise that much money?" the lawyer asked gently. "Perhaps your aunt or uncle . . ."

Elisabet thought about the reward Aunt Augustine had promised to whoever found the missing map. *I must find the map*, she thought. *It's my only hope for buying Papa's freedom!*

"It's possible that my aunt . . ." She hesitated. She didn't want Mr. Robinson to know that her hopes for her father's rescue were pinned on a mysterious missing map. "I might be able to obtain it," she finished.

"Why don't you talk to your aunt?" Mr. Robinson suggested. "If she is willing to try to ransom your father, you and she can come back here together. Then we could pursue the matter further."

"In the meantime, sir, could you find out if my father is on the *Sophie?*" Elisabet asked. "I would feel so much better if I knew for sure."

Mr. Robinson looked at Elisabet's pleading eyes. "Very well," he said finally. "I'll try my best. Where are you staying if I have any news for you?"

"The Horn of Plenty Bakery," Elisabet said. "My aunt, Madame DuMaurier, is the owner."

"Ah, yes, I know the place," Mr. Robinson said. "That's just a few blocks from here, and they make delicious raisin *roulés*. Well, you'd better return home. It is getting late. My coachman will walk you home. If I have news for you, I will let you know."

CHAPTER 7
FOOTSTEPS DOWNSTAIRS

 The sun was setting as Elisabet patted Brutus and Caesar one more time and headed home, with the coachman walking by her side. She wondered whether Claude and Marie had been worried by her absence. *I hope they won't be angry*, she thought.

When they reached the Horn of Plenty, the coachman tipped his hat and strode off down the street. Elisabet took a deep breath and opened the bakery door.

The bell on the door jangled. Marie, who was behind the counter, looked up with the smile and cheerful "*Bonjour*" she gave every customer. But the smile and greeting disappeared as soon as she saw Elisabet.

"Oh, it is you," Marie said, her face suddenly blank.

"Yes, I'm sorry I was gone so long," Elisabet began, "but I had to—"

"Claude is in the kitchen," Marie interrupted. "Go talk

to him." Marie turned her back on Elisabet and began to rearrange the shelves.

Feeling like a student who has been sent to the school's headmistress, Elisabet made her way back to the kitchen. She found Claude cleaning the counters. His eyebrows knit fiercely as he saw her walk in, but he said nothing. Quickly, her words running together, Elisabet explained where she had been. "I know you told me not to leave," she finished, "but my father's life depended on it. I had to go."

For a long time Claude was silent as he continued to work. Finally, he looked up. "We needed your help in the bakery today, Elisabet. Instead, you were not here. We worried that something had happened to you. I sent Raoul and Marie out to look for you, and that put us even further behind."

"I'm sorry, but—" Elisabet began.

Claude cut her off. "Perhaps you truly believed you had to do this for your father. We all must do what we think is best. But never again leave without telling us where you are going. Do you understand?"

Elisabet hung her head. "Yes, I understand," she said, and this time she meant it.

"Good," he nodded. "Now go help Marie sweep up the shop. We will eat soon."

Marie turned her back when Elisabet re-entered the shop. The two girls worked together in stony silence until it was time for supper. During their meal, Marie talked with Claude and Raoul but pointedly ignored Elisabet. When it was time for bed, Marie went straight to her own room and shut the door.

Elisabet, whose turn it was to have the candle, lit her own way upstairs. She stood for a moment on the landing outside Marie's door. Then she gathered her courage and knocked.

"What is it?" Marie asked abruptly.

Elisabet entered the room. Marie, who had been sitting on her bed, stood up and put her hands on her hips. "What do you want?" she demanded.

"I wanted to say . . ." Elisabet hesitated. "I wanted to say that I am sorry. I know my absence today made extra work for you."

Marie's face flushed with anger. "Work!" she exploded. "What do you know about work! Ever since you came here I have been trying to teach you how to work in the bakery, but you do not care at all. You think that because you're Madame's niece, you can take over the whole shop without doing any work!"

Elisabet stepped back, astonished by Marie's fury. "You don't understand. I've never wanted to take over the bakery!"

"Hah!" Marie scoffed. "Do you really expect me to believe that?"

"But it's true," Elisabet protested. "Why, I never even thought of it."

Marie looked at her, eyes full of disbelief. "Who would not want a bakery like this?" she demanded.

Elisabet was dumbfounded. She searched for a way to make Marie understand her. "I don't really care at all about working here. You said so yourself. Can you imagine me owning the bakery?"

This last question caused Marie to hesitate. She looked at Elisabet skeptically. "*Non*, I cannot," she said at last. "But what do you want, then?"

Elisabet sighed. "All I want is to find my father and go back to Boston."

"You mean you would leave New Orleans once you found your father?" Marie asked.

"Of course," said Elisabet. "Boston is my home. It will always be my home. I want to go back there more than I can say."

"Oh," Marie said slowly. She sat down on the edge of her bed. "I suppose I was wrong."

"Did you actually think I wanted to take your place in the bakery?" Elisabet asked.

"Of course," Marie replied. "I have always hoped to make this bakery my own someday. It's been my dream. When you arrived, I thought you would have the same dream."

"But you've been so kind to me," said Elisabet. "I never knew you were angry."

"You are Monsieur DuMaurier's niece," Marie

explained. "I thought he would have wanted me to teach you about the bakery just as he once taught me. Helping you was my gift to him—the last thing I could do for him. But then I saw that you did not care about the bakery. And when you ran off today, I told myself I would never forgive you. It seemed so unfair that you should inherit what I have always dreamed of."

"*My* dream is for Papa to be freed and for us to sail back to Boston together," Elisabet assured her. "That's all I've ever wanted."

"You miss your father very much, *non?*" Marie asked.

"Yes," said Elisabet quietly. She sat down on a corner of Marie's bed. "My mother died when I was five. Since then, it's just been Papa and me. Papa often had to go on long voyages, but I always knew when he was going to come back. When I was small, he'd count out pebbles for me and put them in a jar. Every day he was away, I would take one pebble out of the jar. When the jar was almost empty, I knew he would soon be home.

"When I was older, I would mark each day on a calendar. As the time came near for him to return, I'd rush home from school each afternoon and check for any word or sighting of his ship.

"Sometimes he'd be late," she continued. "One year he told me he would be home by mid-November. I watched every day for him, but he didn't come. I drove our housekeeper quite mad by asking about him. December came and I couldn't even think about Christmas. All I wanted was Papa's return. Yet there was no word of his ship anywhere. I went to bed that Christmas Eve crying.

"Then, in the middle of the night, I heard the door open downstairs and our housekeeper say, 'Well, bless my soul, it's Captain Holder!' I ran downstairs and found Papa, covered with snow. His ship had been caught in a storm, and they had been forced to sail into New York for repairs. He'd traveled by stagecoach all the way from New York just so he could be home for Christmas with me. And he brought me my doll, Agnes."

Elisabet stopped for a moment, then said in a trembling voice, "When they told me Papa wasn't coming home this time, that he'd been taken prisoner, I couldn't believe it. I miss him so much."

Marie bit her lip in thought. "I cannot imagine what it must be like to be rich enough to have a housekeeper or go to school," she said. "But I do know what it is like to miss a father."

In a quiet voice, Marie explained that she had never known her real father or mother. "I was left on the steps of the convent when I was a baby. There was no note, just a baby wrapped in a yellow blanket. The nuns raised me until I was seven. Then one day the DuMauriers came to the convent looking for a girl to sweep up around the bakery. I was little, but I wanted to have a real job, so I told them I was the best sweeper in New Orleans.

"I was lucky to find a home here," Marie continued. "The DuMauriers have always been kind, especially Monsieur DuMaurier. One time, I was so sick I could not eat. Monsieur made me caudles, special soups for the sick. I remember him saying, 'Come, you must drink these caudles so you will grow strong again.' Then he fed me spoonful by spoonful, until I was well enough to feed myself.

"On Sundays, we would go to church together, and he would read to me from his big English Bible. Then, if it was nice, we'd go for a walk. If it was raining, we'd play chess. Sometimes, he even took me to the theater."

Marie paused, and then she added almost to herself, "Monsieur DuMaurier was like a father to me. I will never forget him."

"Maybe we're more alike than we realized," Elisabet suggested. "If my uncle was like a father to you, then we should be cousins!"

Marie smiled. "I'm sorry I lost my temper," she apologized. "Monsieur DuMaurier always said I was hotheaded."

"We really are alike!" Elisabet exclaimed. "Papa always said I had a fiery temper too, just like my fiery red hair."

The two girls laughed, and the more they talked, the more they found they had in common. They both loved music and animals—especially dogs. They were both scared of lightning and spiders.

"And ever since I came here, I have been scared of the

noises I hear at night," said Elisabet. "I know Claude says it's probably rats, but the cat he borrowed didn't catch any rats. Besides, I've heard rats before, and that's not what they sounded like."

Marie looked down at her hands. "I have a confession to make. I have heard some strange noises as well. Not on the night you heard them—I slept soundly that whole night—but on other nights, before you arrived here. The same nights our neighbors said they saw the ghost."

"Why didn't you say something?"

"Claude does not like us to speak of ghosts," said Marie. "He thinks it is foolishness. And I knew Raoul would laugh at me. Besides, if it is Monsieur DuMaurier's ghost, perhaps he is searching for something, something he must find."

"What if it's not a ghost making the noises?" asked Elisabet. "What if it's that awful man, Lucas McCain? He said he'd come back."

"I wondered about that," Marie said. "But then I remembered that Monsieur McCain told us he had been away. He said he had just returned to New Orleans and learned about the map."

"How does that matter?"

"The noises started weeks before Monsieur McCain came to threaten us at the bakery. I first heard them just after Madame DuMaurier went to Baton Rouge."

"Mr. McCain might have been lying," Elisabet suggested.

"You said yourself he was a snake."

"Yes, but he would not have had any reason to lie about that," Marie reasoned. "And if he had known about the map, he probably would have tried to get it from us as soon as he could. Why wait for weeks?"

For a moment the two girls sat in silence in the small, dark room lit only by the single candle. Finally, Elisabet said, "You really think it is a ghost, don't you?"

Marie bit her lip. Then she nodded.

"Why do you think my Uncle Henri would come back to haunt us? Do you suppose it has something to do with his map?"

"I do not know, but yes, I think it is possible," Marie said. "What else could it be?"

Elisabet shivered. "Perhaps . . ." She hesitated. "Perhaps my uncle is angry at me. Perhaps he doesn't want me here."

"He invited you here," said Marie. "He told me so himself."

"Yes, but . . ." Elisabet paused and then decided to ask a question she had been wondering about. "Did my uncle ever talk about my mother? Did he say what she was like?"

"He did not say very much," Marie replied. "He was older than she, and he told me he left home when your mother was still little. He did say she was a pretty child with a will as strong as the Mississippi River."

"What did he mean by that?"

Marie thought for a moment. "I think his exact words were 'Just like the river, once she decided to go a certain way there was no changing her mind.'"

"My mother's family was upset when she decided to marry Papa and move to Boston," Elisabet said thoughtfully. "I wonder if they ever forgave her."

"I do not know," said Marie, "but when Monsieur DuMaurier received your letter, he seemed pleased you were coming. He said it would be good for me to have someone my own age at the bakery and—"

Suddenly, Marie broke off. "Wait," she whispered. "Do you hear that?"

Elisabet listened but heard nothing. After a while Marie shrugged. "I thought I heard a noise downstairs, but perhaps I was just imagining it. Sometimes at night I hear all kinds of things."

"I do, too. In fact, I've often wished I'd accepted your offer to sleep in here."

"Bring in your things!" Marie invited her.

So that night, both girls snuggled comfortably in Marie's bed. Elisabet cuddled her doll Agnes, and she noticed that Marie held tight to a small, tattered yellow blanket.

Marie saw Elisabet looking at the blanket. "This is the blanket I was found in," she confided. "The nuns let me keep it. When I hold it, it makes me happy, because I think maybe my mother once touched it, too."

I haven't found Papa yet, Elisabet thought. *But I have*

made a friend. For the first time in months, she went to sleep feeling at peace.

In the middle of the night, however, Elisabet awoke suddenly. She knew instantly that a noise had disturbed her. She looked over at Marie, to see if she had heard anything, but her friend was still sleeping.

For a few minutes, Elisabet lay in bed listening. Had there really been a noise? she wondered. Then she heard the unmistakable sounds of heavy footsteps and creaking floorboards. The noises were coming from the second floor—the DuMauriers' empty apartment.

Heart pounding, she nudged Marie. "Wake up!" she whispered.

"What?" Marie mumbled sleepily.

"Shhhhh! Listen!"

Marie half sat up in bed. She grasped Elisabet's arm, and together the two girls listened to the sounds of more footsteps, then a thump.

Elisabet felt herself shaking with fear. These footsteps sounded much louder than the noises she had heard before—and terrifyingly close.

She whispered to Marie, "Do you think we should go downstairs to see what's happening?"

Marie shook her head. "*Non.* Do you?"

"No," Elisabet agreed, immensely relieved. "But what should we do?"

"We could block the door," Marie whispered.

Quietly, both girls slipped under the mosquito netting and out of bed. They picked up Marie's wooden chair and propped it under the handle of the door. Then they jumped back into bed. Elisabet, still shaking, clutched Agnes, and Marie hugged her yellow blanket. They heard several more thumps, but the noises seemed to be growing fainter. Then they heard the sound of a door closing. All became quiet.

For a long time, both girls lay in bed, sometimes whispering and wondering what the noises could have been, sometimes just listening. After a while, though, the pauses in their conversation became longer and longer.

Then Elisabet heard a gentle snoring, and she knew her friend had dropped off to sleep. Elisabet tried to stay awake and on guard for both of them, but sleep finally conquered her, too.

At breakfast, the girls told Claude and Raoul about the mysterious noises they had heard in the night.

"Don't tell me you believe in all the ghost stories," Raoul laughed. "I thought you were too brave for that."

"It may not have been a ghost," Marie snapped. "But something was there. We both heard it."

Claude frowned at them. "No fighting. We have work to do. I will check the building to see if anyone broke in." He left the kitchen, but soon he was back.

"The doors and windows are locked, and nothing appears to have been stolen," he told the girls. "Would you feel better if Raoul slept in the kitchen tonight?"

"No one could get past the great Raoul!" the skinny boy bragged.

Elisabet and Marie looked at Raoul, then at each other. They both shook their heads. "*Merci*, but no," said Marie.

"Very well," said Claude. "Remember, all houses creak at night. A few noises are nothing to worry about. Don't let your imaginations run away with you. And no more talk about ghosts—it will give the bakery a bad name."

CHAPTER 8
TREASURE SEARCH

C offee, girl!"
"Another roll, if you please."
"A dozen raisin *roulés*—and hurry!"
"More coffee!"

All morning, customers kept Elisabet and Marie so busy they barely had time to catch their breath, much less discuss the events of the previous night. When the morning's rush finally ended, the two girls looked at each other.

"I know Claude doesn't believe us, but someone was in the apartment last night," Elisabet said.

"What can we do, though?" said Marie. "We have no proof!"

"If only—" Elisabet began, but she was interrupted by the jangling of the bell on the front door. She looked up and saw the plump blond girl, Caroline, entering with her father.

"I'll go get more breads," Marie whispered to Elisabet.

"You take care of the customers."

Elisabet nodded, then turned to Caroline and her father. "*Bonjour*," she greeted them. Neither Caroline nor her father returned her greeting.

"I don't know what I want today, Papa," Caroline said, eyeing the pastries critically. "Nothing looks very good."

Although she kept a smile on her face, Elisabet felt outraged. *All our pastries are delicious!* she thought. *How dare this girl insult Claude's baking!*

"You had best eat something before your French lesson, Caroline," the father said. He studied the shelves for a moment, then pointed to a cheese pastry. "We'll take one of those," he announced. He handed Elisabet a silver dollar.

She gave him his change, and the father and daughter walked away, arm in arm.

They never even say good morning to me, Elisabet thought resentfully, as she watched the father and daughter stroll down the street. *It is as if I am not even a person, just a part of the bakery.*

Sadly, she realized that Caroline and her father didn't see Miss Elisabet Holder, daughter of Captain John Holder. All they saw was a young shop assistant who they felt was unworthy of their attention. *When I get back to Boston, I will never forget what it is like to be a shop assistant*, Elisabet promised herself. *And I will always, always say good morning to the people who wait on me. But how will I get back to Boston?*

Elisabet was deep in thought when Marie returned to the bakery with a tray filled with fragrant, hot loaves of bread. "What is wrong?" Marie asked her. "You look worried."

"I was thinking about the treasure map," Elisabet said. "I *have* to find it. It's my only hope of raising enough money to ransom my father."

Marie shook her head. "I would like to help you, but we've already looked everywhere."

"What about our floor—the third floor?"

"We searched every inch," Marie assured her. "There's not much up there, you know."

"That's true," Elisabet agreed thoughtfully. "Uncle Henri said 'upstairs,' so if his map is not on the third floor, it has to be in the apartment somewhere."

"We mustn't go up there," Marie said in a low voice. "Madame DuMaurier left strict instructions that no one was to enter her apartment."

"No one?"

Marie thought for a moment. "She did ask Claude to water the flowers while she was away. But that is all."

"Someone was up there last night," Elisabet protested. "We both heard it. Could that have been Claude?"

"Of course not," said Marie. "He would have told us. Besides, he only goes up there in the afternoons."

"Well, whoever was there last night may come back another night—and they may find the treasure map before we can," Elisabet persisted. "Oh, I wish I could go up right now and look around."

"It is no good looking during the day," Marie reminded her. "Monsieur DuMaurier said to 'search in the night.'"

"Could we get in tonight? Is it locked?"

"It is locked," Marie whispered. She looked around the bakery and made sure it was empty. "But I know how to get in. We'll start after dinner. Not a word to anyone, though, not even Claude. Promise?"

"I promise."

After dinner, Elisabet and Marie announced they were so tired they were going to bed early. The two girls said good night, climbed the stairs, and then waited nervously in the room they now shared. First, they heard Raoul leave. Then they heard the jingle of keys as Claude carefully locked up the bakery. Finally, the front door closed and they could hear Claude whistling as he walked home to his family.

"I think we're safe now," Marie said quietly.

Elisabet hesitated. During the day, it had seemed like a good idea to search the apartment. But now that it was dark, she dreaded the thought of walking into the empty rooms downstairs. What would they find there? Would someone—or something—be waiting for them?

Marie seemed to share her thoughts. "We do not have to go tonight," she suggested. "Perhaps another evening, when we end work earlier . . ."

Elisabet was tempted. Then she thought of Papa, imprisoned on a British ship. *I won't disappoint you, Papa*, she resolved. *I'll be as brave as you are.* She swallowed her fears. "We must go now," she told Marie. "You said yourself we have to search in the night. Come on."

Picking up the candle, Elisabet led the way down the dark, winding stairs. The candle's flame cast eerie shadows on the walls, and with each step, Elisabet wanted to turn back. But she forced herself to keep going. When they finally reached the apartment door, both girls stood for a moment on the landing, listening. All was silent.

Then Marie whispered, "Help me up. The key is on top of the door."

Elisabet put down the candle, then leaned over and clasped her hands so they made a stirrup for Marie's foot. "Hold on to my shoulder," Elisabet whispered back. "One, two . . . three!"

Pushing hard, Elisabet hoisted Marie so she could reach the ledge above the door. With her free hand, Marie felt along the dusty ledge. "I can't find it . . . wait . . . here it is!" Triumphantly, Marie held up a long key, and Elisabet lowered her to the floor.

"Monsieur DuMaurier always kept an extra key up there," Marie explained. She put the big key in the lock and turned it. The door creaked open. The girls looked at each other, then cautiously ventured inside.

Elisabet found herself in the parlor of the two-room

apartment. By the light of their candle, she could see a room full of furniture, with several bookcases lining the walls. The room was hot, but it did not have the stuffy, closed-up odor Elisabet had expected. "It smells like flowers in here," she noted with surprise.

"Perhaps Claude had the doors to the balcony open earlier," said Marie.

She crossed over to a set of tall French windows, which opened like double doors onto a small balcony that overlooked the street. She unlocked the double doors and walked out onto the balcony, which was filled with window boxes full of roses.

"They were Monsieur DuMaurier's favorite flowers," Marie recalled, looking wistfully at the red blooms.

Elisabet walked over to the French windows and squinted out into the darkened street. She saw a man standing in the shadows of a building across the street, smoking a cigar. Although she could not see him clearly, she could tell he was a big man. An image of Lucas McCain crossed her mind. "I wonder who that is," she said.

"Probably someone who lives on this street," suggested Marie. "Maybe he is waiting for a friend."

"Maybe," replied Elisabet doubtfully. She had an odd feeling of being watched, but she could not explain why. "Let's go back inside. We shouldn't let anyone see us up here."

The two girls walked back inside, shutting the French

windows behind them and closing the faded, rose-colored curtains. Now it was even darker in the apartment, and the candle's dim light left the rest of the room in deep shadows.

Elisabet had a sudden, frightening thought. *What if someone is already in here with us?* She felt a shiver crawl up her spine.

"Let's check the rooms before we begin searching," she whispered to Marie.

Candle held high, the girls carefully examined the parlor. Elisabet took special notice of a large, rose-colored settee that sat with its back to the window, facing the fireplace at the other end of the room. It was so big that someone could easily hide behind it. She gathered up her courage and peered around it. There was no one.

In front of the settee stood a small mahogany table with a chess set on top. Two armchairs flanked the table, creating a sitting nook for talking or playing chess. As Elisabet checked behind the farthest chairs, the floor creaked loudly, and Elisabet started. But no one was there.

Elisabet was just starting to feel a little more comfortable when she heard a loud *Ding! Ding!* She jumped, and then stifled a scream as hot candle wax dripped on her arm.

"What was that?"

Marie smiled and pointed to a wooden clock that stood on top of the fireplace mantel. "It scared me, too," she confessed. "Claude must have wound it today when he was checking the apartment."

Elisabet felt her heart pounding from the fright. She paused for a moment and took a deep breath. Then she pointed to a door. "What's back there?"

"The bedroom," Marie whispered.

Together, the two girls quietly entered the smaller of the two rooms and checked under the four-poster bed. Elisabet looked around the room. It was tightly filled with furniture, including a large mahogany dresser with a mirror above it, a washstand, a small writing desk, and a straight chair. Other than under the bed, she saw no place where an intruder could hide.

There is no one here, Elisabet told herself firmly. *So why do I feel as if someone is watching me?*

A door in the back of the room led to the outside landing and stairs that went down to the courtyard. She checked to be sure the door was locked. Then she turned to Marie. "Where should we search first?"

"We might as well begin in here," Marie said. "But remember, we have looked through all this before, so don't be surprised if we find nothing."

By the wavering light of their candle, the girls peered under the mattress, lifted the carpet, checked the papers in the writing desk, and searched behind the washstand and the dresser. All they found were a few odds and ends—a button, scraps of paper, a few coins—but nothing that seemed as if it could be a map or even a clue to the map's whereabouts. They worked carefully and tried to put everything back exactly as they found it.

As they searched, it grew more windy outside, and the old building started to creak and sway slightly. The chiming clock had just struck midnight when they heard a loud bang from the parlor.

Both girls jumped. Then they sat in silence, looking at each other in the flickering candlelight, waiting for another noise.

"What do you think that was?" Marie whispered, clenching the candle tight in her hands.

Elisabet mouthed the words "I don't know." Fear gripped her stomach. For a long time, they listened for more noises. As they sat, Elisabet felt a cooling breeze blow through the room. "Are the windows open?" she whispered to Marie.

"*Non*, we closed them."

On her hands and knees, Elisabet crawled toward the door that led from the bedroom to the parlor. She could see the rose-colored curtains blowing through the open window.

"They are open now," she whispered. "Do you think we should go look?"

Marie swallowed. Then she nodded. Slowly, the girls got up and inched their way through the parlor. Elisabet felt every muscle tense. She was ready to scream and run at the first sign of danger. But nothing in the parlor appeared to be changed except the open windows.

As they approached, there was a sudden gust of wind, and the French windows opened wide, banging against the walls and making the same sound they had heard before.

Marie gave a nervous laugh. "I'm glad it was just the wind," she said. "I suppose we didn't close the windows tightly enough." She firmly yanked the double windows' lock in place. "There. That should keep them shut."

Elisabet was peering through the curtains. Across the street, she could see the vague outline of a man standing by a building and the red embers of his cigar, burning brightly. She grabbed Marie's arm. "Look, that man we saw before—I think he's still there."

Marie peeked out the curtains. "How do you know it is the same man?" she asked. "Maybe it is someone else. Or maybe he is still waiting for his friend. In any case, he is not bothering us."

"I suppose you're right," Elisabet agreed reluctantly. "Let's get back to work."

The girls tried to continue their search of the bedroom. But their fright—combined with their long day's work—had left them both exhausted.

Marie yawned widely. "Let's go to bed," she said. "We have done enough searching for one night. I am so tired I could not find the map now if it fell in front of me."

"I'm tired, too," Elisabet admitted. "We'll have to come back tomorrow night."

Before the girls locked up the apartment, Elisabet took one last look out at the street. It now seemed deserted.

"I don't see that man now," she told Marie.

"*Bien!*" her friend said, grabbing her elbow. "Now let's sleep."

As she and Marie climbed the narrow stairs to their little room on the top floor, Elisabet looked down the winding staircase behind them. All she could see was darkness. Yet she could not rid herself of the powerful feeling that she was being watched.

Chapter 9
Disturbing News

The next morning in the bakery, all the customers were talking about the latest news: Pierre Lafitte, brother of Jean Lafitte, had escaped last night from the New Orleans jail!

"What will those Lafittes do next?" one woman clucked.

"I'd wager my last coin that Jean Lafitte paid those jailers to let Pierre walk free," an older man declared.

Listening to the gossip, Elisabet grew more and more concerned. With Pierre out of jail, perhaps Jean Lafitte would no longer need a lawyer's help. What would happen to Mr. Robinson? Would the lawyer still be able to find out whether Papa was aboard the *Sophie*?

When Elisabet went back to the kitchen, she told Claude about her concerns. The big baker shrugged. "Jean Lafitte has no more need of a lawyer for Pierre, perhaps. But his problems with the law are far from over. I am sure he will still work with your friend Monsieur Robinson on other matters."

Elisabet wished she could feel so confident. *What if Mr. Robinson never talked to Jean Lafitte again? Would she ever discover what had happened to Papa?*

Marie came hurrying into the kitchen. "*Pardon*, Claude. There is a man in the shop who is planning a party for tonight. He wants to place a very big order. I thought you should talk with him."

Claude dried his hands on his apron and went across the courtyard to the bakery. In a few minutes, he was back with the news that they would all need to work late that night. "It seems some friends of the Lafittes will join together tonight to celebrate Pierre's escape. They want our best cakes for their gathering."

Elisabet was horrified. "The pirates won't be at the party, will they?"

"No," Claude said. "Even the Lafittes would not dare to come out quite that openly. This is a party for their friends—which include some of our city's leading citizens. We had better get busy!"

The small staff worked hard throughout the day. When the shop was not busy, Elisabet helped out in the sweltering kitchen. With Marie to guide her, she chopped ingredients and mixed dough. Everyone was so busy they even skipped their siesta. They took only a quick dinner, then went back to work.

When the two girls were in the bakery alone together, Elisabet quietly asked her friend, "Do you think we will have time to search tonight?"

Marie brushed a lock of hair from her sweating forehead. "*Non*, on special days like this we always work quite late. We will have to wait until tomorrow."

Elisabet nodded, disappointed that they must wait, but also secretly relieved she would not have to return to the apartment that evening.

By the time all the cakes were ready for the party, the sun had set. Claude stacked the desserts on three large wooden trays and gave Raoul directions to the house where the party was scheduled to take place.

"You and the girls take these over there while I clean up," Claude said. "Be careful now, and do not drop anything."

As they walked outside into the clear, moonlit night, Elisabet checked the street. She could see no sign of McCain or anyone who resembled the heavyset man. Elisabet breathed a sigh of relief, and her spirits rose. It was exciting to see the city at night! Laughter, light, and tempting smells filtered out the windows from cafés, and vendors all along the street called out to them as they passed.

"Ginger beer, fresh cool ginger beer!"

"Pralines! Sweet pecan pralines!"

The house where the party was being given was only

three blocks from the bakery. Just as Elisabet's arms were getting tired from carrying the heavy tray, Raoul entered a courtyard and knocked at the back door of a large, elegant home.

A young maid opened the door. "Come in, come in," she said. "Those sure look good! Put them on that long table over there."

As she unloaded her tray, Elisabet caught a glimpse of the front rooms of the house, which were aglow with hundreds of candles. At first, she was startled to see a man dressed like a Roman warrior waltzing with a young lady who looked like a princess. Then she realized that this was a costume ball. Violinists were playing a lively tune, while men and women in all kinds of fancy costumes were dancing, laughing, and talking loudly. Elisabet saw a beautiful woman dressed like the French queen Marie Antoinette and wearing a tiara of diamonds. She was laughing with a man in a powdered wig and old-fashioned knee breeches.

So the pirate Jean Lafitte really does have friends among the wealthy people here, Elisabet thought. *How strange this city is!* Suddenly, Elisabet caught a glimpse of a man who looked a great deal like Mr. Robinson. *Could he be here?* she wondered. She began to walk toward the dining room to try to get a better look at the man, but the young maid shooed her away.

"You don't belong out here with the quality, girl," the maid whispered, looking at Elisabet's dirty bare feet, mosquito-bitten arms, and worn work shift. "Get back into the kitchen!"

Reluctantly, Elisabet followed the maid to the back of the house. Soon she, Marie, and Raoul were heading back toward the bakery with their now-empty trays. They paused by the praline vendor, and Elisabet curiously sniffed the sweet smell of brown sugar, nuts, and butter. She had seen people eating the flat, round candies set with pecans, but she had never tried one.

"Claude gave me money so we could buy pralines," Raoul announced. "I don't want to buy mine now, but you girls can get yours."

The girls each ordered two of the large pralines, and Elisabet discovered that the rich pecan candies were delicious. She eagerly devoured her whole treat.

Marie, however, ate only one of hers. "I am full," she told Raoul. She handed him the other praline. "Take this one to your sisters and brothers."

"*Merci*," he said, wrapping the candy in his handkerchief and pocketing it. He looked so grateful Elisabet wished she had saved him some, too. But if Raoul had wanted a praline, why hadn't he bought his own?

Later, when the two girls were up in their room together, she asked Marie, "Why did you give Raoul your praline? Were you really full?"

"*Non*, but I knew he was saving his candy money to give to his mother. He tries to give her every penny he can. He does not like to let people know, though."

As she lay in bed that night, Elisabet hugged her doll. *This is a very strange city, Agnes,* she thought. *Rich people have parties for outlaws, while poor people like Raoul work hard and save every penny. And here I am searching for a map made by a smuggler!*

If there were noises that night, both girls were so tired they slept through them. The next morning, Elisabet was busy restocking the shelves with hot loaves of French bread when she heard a familiar voice. "May I have two raisin *roulés*, please?"

She looked up in surprise. "Mr. Robinson!"

She handed him the *roulés*, and as he paid her he said quietly, "I have news for you. Why don't we sit for a moment?"

Elisabet looked around the bakery. Fortunately, it was almost time for the midday break and most of the customers had already left. Marie was serving the last two ladies, and now she nodded to Elisabet as if to say, "Go talk with him!"

Wiping her hands nervously on her work shift, Elisabet sat down with Mr. Robinson at the farthest little table. "What have you heard?" she asked anxiously.

In a low voice, Mr. Robinson said, "As a favor to me,

Jean Lafitte relayed a message to the *Sophie* asking
whether they had the American, Captain John Holder,
aboard."

"And do they?"

The lawyer nodded. "Yes. They said they would be
willing to release him as a 'goodwill gesture,' but it would
cost a great deal of money."

"How much?"

Mr. Robinson looked at her sadly. "I'm sorry, Elisabet.
They are demanding three thousand dollars. Not a penny
less."

Elisabet was stunned. "But I thought you said two
thousand," she protested.

"That was my estimate," he admitted. "I have a
feeling the British are being hardheaded because they feel
Monsieur Lafitte is not helping them sufficiently."

"It's so much money!" Elisabet said.

"I'm afraid there's more bad news," Mr. Robinson said.
"The *Sophie* probably will not stay here much longer. Soon
her captain will want to rejoin the British fleet."

He paused and looked around the modest bakery.
"Elisabet, I realize this is difficult for you. But you mustn't
feel too bad. Your father would never expect you to be
able to raise that much money."

"I *will* find the money somehow," Elisabet declared.
"I just don't know how yet."

"I wish you the best, my dear," Mr. Robinson said,

patting her on the hand. Then he rose to his feet. "Now I must go. You are welcome to visit anytime—my dogs Brutus and Caesar took a great fancy to you. Good-bye, and good luck."

As soon as Mr. Robinson left, Marie hurried over. "What did he say?" she demanded. "Is there news of your father?"

Elisabet quickly recounted her conversation. When she told Marie about the ransom amount, the dark-haired girl gave a low whistle. "Three thousand dollars!" she declared. "It might as well be three million."

"We must find the treasure map," Elisabet whispered to her friend.

"We will look tonight," Marie agreed.

As soon as Raoul and Claude left that evening, the girls prepared to return to the empty apartment. They both dreaded the task.

"I used to love visiting the apartment," Marie confessed, as they heard Claude lock the doors. "Now I hate it there. Ever since Monsieur DuMaurier died, the rooms seem different somehow, unfriendly."

"I don't like it either," said Elisabet. "I wish we had something to protect ourselves with."

Marie reached under her bed and pulled out a large, heavy rolling pin. "I borrowed it from the kitchen tonight," she said with a shy smile. "If we return it first thing in the morning, Claude will never know it was gone."

"What a wonderful idea!" Elisabet exclaimed. "I wish I had thought of it."

Marie held the rolling pin tightly as the two girls crept down the stairs together, alert to every sound in the house. They paused on the landing and listened intently. All was quiet.

With Elisabet's help, Marie reached up and retrieved the key above the door. Then they slowly opened the door and, candle held high, checked for any sign of movement in the dark parlor. "It looks all right," Elisabet whispered.

Marie nodded and locked the door behind them. When the bolt fell into place with a click, Elisabet felt a sinking feeling in her stomach. *I hope everything is all right,* she thought to herself, *because now we're locked in.*

Marie must have had the same thought. "I will leave the key in the lock," she whispered to Elisabet, "in case we need to leave quickly."

With the rolling pin poised for attack, the two girls looked behind all the big furniture in the two rooms. When they were satisfied that no one could be hiding in the apartment, they began to relax slightly.

"Let's start in the parlor tonight," Elisabet suggested. "I want to look through those bookcases. Perhaps Uncle Henri hid his map in one of the books."

The girls decided to begin with the bookcases on either side of the settee. Carefully, they took down each book in turn and looked through its pages. It was slow work.

"My uncle had a great many books," Elisabet noted, as the pile of examined books grew larger and larger.

"He loved to read," said Marie. "When he was rich, he bought many books. It was the only part of his treasure he did not give to the church. He said the nuns would not have much use for his books, but he would."

Suddenly, Marie broke off. "Wait," she whispered to Elisabet. "Do you hear that?"

Elisabet listened. There was a creaking noise, as if someone were coming up the outside stairs. "Hide!" she whispered, and she blew out the candle.

Marie grabbed the rolling pin and scrambled behind the drapes that hid the French window. Elisabet crouched behind the settee. Hearts beating wildly, they waited while the creaking came closer. They heard what sounded like a door opening in the bedroom.

Elisabet felt herself shaking with fear. She sent up a silent prayer. *O Lord in heaven, protect us. Please!*

The footsteps came closer and closer. Terrified, Elisabet peered around the corner of the settee. She stifled a gasp as she saw what was coming through the door. It was a tall, white, ghostly figure carrying a single candle—and it was coming toward her!

CHAPTER 10
A GHOSTLY VISITOR

The ghostly figure moved slowly, haltingly, across the room. It was almost as tall as a man, but it had no distinct head, arms, or legs. It was a flow of white, lit up by the one gleaming candle.

By the light of the ghost's candle, Elisabet could see the books she had left piled on the floor just a few feet away from her hiding place. How foolish she had been to leave them out! Now the ghost would know someone had been in the apartment.

Her only hope was escape, but how? The ghost was coming right toward her, and the apartment door was locked. Where could she go? And what about Marie? Even if she herself could escape, she could not leave her friend alone and unprotected.

Elisabet shifted her balance slightly to try to see where Marie was hiding behind the curtains. The old floor creaked beneath her as she moved. She froze in fear.

The ghost stopped, too, as if listening. Then the white figure moved even closer to her hiding place. Elisabet desperately wanted to scream, but she was terrified that the ghost would discover her. She bit her lip hard.

Another noise came from the area by the French window. *Marie?* Elisabet thought. The ghost turned and started moving toward the window. Just as it was about to pass Elisabet, however, it seemed to stumble over the pile of books on the floor. As it tottered, its candle flickered. In the last light of the candle, Elisabet saw the white figure lunge toward her in the darkness.

"No!" she screamed. "*No!*"

She bolted for the door, but the ghost had fallen in her way, and she found herself entangled with it. Together, they crashed into the table and knocked over the chess set.

"Let me go!" she screamed, kicking with all her might and struggling to free herself from the white figure that covered her. "Let me go!"

Marie leaped out from behind the curtain and joined the fight, pounding on the ghost with her fists and trying to help Elisabet pull away.

"*Zut alors!*" the ghost cried. "Stop!"

Through all her fear, Elisabet slowly became aware that the ghost—if ghost it was—sounded somehow familiar. When Marie had jumped from her hiding place to help her friend, she had left the curtains open, and now the room was dimly lit by the moon outside. As Elisabet finally succeeded in pulling folds of white material from her face, she could faintly see the eyes of the ghostly figure staring back at her. Suddenly, she knew where she had heard that voice before.

"Raoul?" she asked in amazement. "Is that you?"

Raoul slowly got to his feet, pulling off a white sheet as he did so. "*Oui*," he said sheepishly.

Marie gasped. "*Raoul!*" she cried. Then she pummeled him again. "*You* are the ghost! You idiot! You scared us to death!"

"I'm sorry," Raoul said, backing away from the angry Marie. "You scared me, too. I did not know you were here."

"It's a good thing for you that I did not hit you with my rolling pin!" Marie exclaimed. "I had it ready, but I was afraid of hitting Elisabet."

"Has it been you all along?" Elisabet felt both angry and relieved. "Have you been the ghost?"

Raoul nodded. "I was here looking for the treasure map, same as you, I guess. I have never found anything, though. Have you?"

"*Non*, but you could have told us what you were doing. We could have worked together," Marie said. She took a tinderbox from the mantel and relit their candles. "Why this playacting?"

"I wanted to find it on my own so I could get the reward from Madame DuMaurier," Raoul admitted. "My mother could surely use that money."

"But you attacked me!" Elisabet said, still trying to get her breath back from the fight.

"I did not attack you," Raoul protested. "I never meant to hurt anyone. I tripped over those books on the floor. It was you who attacked me!"

"Why did you pretend to be a ghost?" Elisabet asked.

"When the neighbors started saying they saw a ghost over here, I knew they must have noticed my candle at night. At first I was scared I would be caught. Then I thought, why not dress up like a ghost? That way, no one would know who I was."

"How did you get in?" Marie asked, still angry and suspicious.

"I know where Madame DuMaurier keeps a spare key to the back door. I borrowed it and came up the outside stairs." Raoul paused. "How did *you* get in?" he asked. "You are not supposed to be here either."

"Never mind," scolded Marie. "Besides, we were not the ones who dressed up like a ghost. We never scared anyone."

"That's true," Elisabet said. "You terrified us the other night—and then you laughed at us for believing in ghosts."

"That was strange," Raoul replied. "I know you said you heard something, but it was not me. My mother needed me at home that night. I never came back here."

Elisabet and Marie looked at each other, the same thought running through their minds: *If Raoul didn't make the noises the other night, who did?* Then Marie turned back to Raoul. "Are you telling us the truth?" she demanded.

"I swear," he said solemnly. "When you said you heard a ghost, I thought you had just started to take the stories too seriously. What did you hear, really?"

The girls described the noises they had heard—noises that sounded exactly like footsteps coming from the apartment.

"I do not know who it was," he said, looking around the dark apartment nervously. "But it was not me. I had better be getting home now. I do not want my mother to discover I am gone."

Raoul picked up his sheet and headed toward the back door. Then he hesitated. "You won't tell anyone that I was the ghost, will you?"

"Will you promise on your grandmother's grave never, ever, to haunt this apartment again?" Marie asked.

"I promise. But you have to promise not to tell anyone it was me."

The girls looked at each other. Then they both nodded agreement.

"*Au revoir,*" said Raoul. "And remember, not a word to anyone."

Raoul left the way he had come, down the outside stairs. Marie carefully locked the door after him. "I wonder who else has a key to the apartment," she murmured.

"Perhaps Claude?" Elisabet suggested. "Could he have

been the person we heard that night? It did sound like a very big man."

"Impossible," said Marie. "I told you, Claude only comes in the afternoons to water the flowers. Besides, he is the most honest person I've ever known. He never would have left us to worry."

Then who? Elisabet wondered. The nasty, sneering face of Lucas McCain came immediately to her mind. *Was that awful man trying to make good on his threats to take the map?*

She went over to the French windows and looked out at the moonlit street. She was thankful she saw no one.

Marie watched her friend. "You believe it is that man Lucas McCain, *non?* You think he is the person we heard."

"I don't know anymore," Elisabet admitted. "I do know we must keep looking for the map. There may not be much more time. Mr. Robinson said the *Sophie* will probably sail in a week or so. If I can't raise the ransom money by then . . ." Elisabet didn't even want to finish the sentence.

"I know, but we are too tired now to keep searching," said Marie. "Let's just straighten up before we go to bed. We will look some more tomorrow."

The girls gathered the books from the floor. Then they picked up the fallen table and looked for the chess pieces that had been scattered by the "ghost." Marie started to set up the board.

"We're still missing two pawns and one knight," she told Elisabet.

Elisabet froze. "What did you say?" she demanded.

"We're still missing two pawns and one knight," Marie repeated. "You know, a knight. That's what they call the chess piece that looks like a horse—a knight." Suddenly Marie gasped. "*Sacrebleu!* Do you think that's what he meant—not 'Search in the night' but 'Search in the knight'?"

"I don't know," Elisabet said excitedly. "Let's find out!"

They searched madly for the missing knight. Finally they found it under the armchair. There didn't seem to be anything unusual about the chess piece. They checked the three other knights, too. All four pieces were the same size, weight, and shape. Two of the knights were black; two were white.

The girls carefully examined each of the pieces by the light of their candle. Elisabet was turning over one of the white pieces when she saw some letters faintly carved on the bottom.

"Marie, look at this!"

"It must be a clue!" Marie exclaimed. "But what does it mean?"

The letters looked like LUKE II XII.

"Could it be someone's name?" Elisabet asked.

"I've never heard of a name like that," said Marie.

The two girls stared at the strange letters. Then Elisabet had an awful thought. "What about Lucas McCain—could 'Luke' refer to 'Lucas'?"

Marie shook her head. "*Non,* Monsieur never mentioned him at all. I never saw or heard of Lucas McCain before that day he appeared in the bakery. The only Luke Monsieur DuMaurier ever talked about was the Luke from the Bible."

"Of course!" said Elisabet. "The Bible—I should have thought of that! Look, these must be Roman numerals. The 'II' stands for 'two' and the 'XII' stands for 'twelve.' I think it means Book of Luke, chapter two, verse twelve."

"Let's go look!" said Marie.

It took only a few minutes for the girls to pull out Monsieur DuMaurier's big, leather-bound English Bible and check the verse. "Here it is," Elisabet pointed eagerly. "It's even marked in pencil."

And this shall be a sign unto you; Ye shall find the babe wrapped in swaddling clothes, lying in a manger.

"What does it mean?" wondered Marie. "Should we look for a baby somewhere?"

For a moment the girls tried to think of all the families they knew who had babies. None of them seemed to have any connection to the missing map.

"Perhaps it's not a real baby," said Elisabet. "Perhaps it's a picture or a statue or something like that."

Marie strode over to the fireplace mantel and took down a small bronze statue of the Madonna and child that stood next to the clock. "This is one of Madame's most prized possessions," she said. "Do you think it could hold the clue we're looking for?"

The girls eagerly checked every inch of the statue. "If there's a clue here, I can't find it," Elisabet said at last. "Are there other statues like this anywhere else?"

"Not that I can think of," said Marie. She yawned. "But I'm so tired I cannot think anymore."

Elisabet had to admit that she, too, was exhausted. Confused and sleepy, the two girls decided it was time to go to bed. Before they walked up the dark stairway, Marie armed herself with the rolling pin, and Elisabet looked carefully up and down the stairs, straining her eyes in the darkness to see if anyone was there. As soon as they were sure the stairway was empty, they hurried up to their room, closing and blocking their door behind them.

Lying in bed that night, Elisabet held Agnes close and thought about the odd letters on the chess piece. *Are they really clues to the mysterious map?* she wondered. *And if so, where could the map be hidden?*

CHAPTER 11
DANGEROUS DISCOVERY

Dawn came early. Much too early. Elisabet rolled over in bed and groaned. "I just fell asleep! It can't be time to wake up already."

"I know," said Marie, who was always first out of bed. "I felt the same way myself. But if we do not get down there soon—"

"We'll miss Claude's breakfast," Elisabet finished for her. Elisabet suddenly discovered she was hungry. Only the tempting thought of Claude's fried pastries and steaming *café au lait* made it possible for her to get out of bed.

The hot coffee was especially welcome today because, for the first time since Elisabet had arrived, it was cool outside, and waves of rain were turning the muddy New Orleans streets into small, fast-moving rivers.

"Will the rain go on like this all day?" Elisabet asked at breakfast.

Claude looked out the window. "By the look of the sky, I'd say so. Perhaps there will be a few breaks, though."

Fortunately for the two tired girls, the driving rain kept most customers away in the morning. Late in the afternoon, however, the weather cleared, although the skies still looked threatening. Customers straggled in, including the blond girl Caroline and her father.

"*Bonjour*," Elisabet welcomed them, in the same tone as she now greeted all customers. "How may I help you?"

Caroline sighed. Today she was wearing a short-sleeved, sky-blue silk dress with a white sash and delicately crocheted white gloves with little pearl buttons. She put her gloves down on the counter as she looked at the full shelves. "I really can't say what I want," she pouted. "I'm tired of those lemon pastries."

"Perhaps you would like some gingerbread, my dear," her father suggested.

"No! I'm tired of that, too." She glanced outside. "Oh, look, Papa, it's beginning to rain again, and my new frock is going to be soiled. Just get me a raisin roll and let's go!"

The father threw Elisabet a coin. "Two raisin rolls," he demanded in his Yankee twang. "And be quick, girl!"

As soon as Elisabet handed them the raisin *roulés*, Caroline and her father hurried off. Elisabet was turning back to her work when she noticed Caroline's gloves lying on the counter.

What a foolish girl! Elisabet thought. *Beautiful gloves like that and she can't even remember to take them with her.* For a moment Elisabet hesitated. Then she picked up the gloves and ran out into the rain. She quickly caught up with Caroline and her father.

"Excuse me! Excuse me!" Elisabet called loudly.

The father turned around and scowled from beneath the umbrella he was carrying. "What is it?" he demanded, looking at Elisabet as if he had never seen her before.

"You left these," said Elisabet, handing the gloves to Caroline.

"Oh, yes, yes," the father mumbled. "Well, here you are then." He reached into his pocket and, pulling out a coin, tossed it at Elisabet. Then he grabbed Caroline's elbow, and the two continued hurrying down the street.

For a moment, Elisabet stood and stared at the coin she had caught by reflex. Then she smiled and pocketed the money. *This isn't charity*, she thought. *I've earned this money. And the next time Marie and I go out, I'm going to buy us a treat—maybe some more of those delicious pralines.*

The shop was so quiet that rainy afternoon that she and Marie had time to talk about the clue on the chess piece.

"Do you think we ought to tell Claude about it? Perhaps he could help us," Marie suggested.

"Yes, but if Claude discovers we've been in the apartment, he might forbid us from ever going back," Elisabet pointed out. "He might even change the lock. Then what would we do?"

"You are right," said Marie. The girls discussed the clue on the chess piece and pondered what it might mean. Should they search for a baby? Or a manger? Or swaddling clothes? Together, Elisabet and Marie considered and rejected dozens of ideas.

"Why ever did Uncle Henri leave such a confusing clue?" Elisabet asked, exasperated.

"I'm not sure," Marie said. "I think he tried to tell me more, but he was not able to. Also . . ."

"What?" Elisabet demanded.

Marie hesitated. Finally she said, "I think he wanted to protect his map. Remember, he said it was important that it not get into the wrong hands."

"But how would a clue written on a chess piece about a Bible verse protect his map?" Elisabet asked.

"The Bible was very important to Monsieur DuMaurier. He read it every day, and he knew much of it by heart," Marie said. "He loved chess, too, and he played it whenever he had a chance. I believe he chose clues that only people who knew him and loved him would understand, because those are the only people he would trust with his map."

"You knew and loved him," Elisabet said. "Do you have any idea where we should look next?"

Marie shook her head. "I have thought about his last

words a thousand times. I believe he was trying very hard to tell me something, but I do not know what it was." Tears welled up in her eyes, and her voice broke. "I feel I have failed him," she confessed.

Elisabet put her arm around her friend. She had been so caught up in her fears for Papa that she had forgotten Marie was still grieving for Monsieur DuMaurier. "I understand," she said gently. "Sometimes I feel I've failed my father, too. But we can't give up. We'll go back to the apartment tonight."

That evening, the two girls again waited until everyone else had left for the day. Then Elisabet armed herself with the rolling pin while Marie held the candle. Together, they crept back to the apartment and carefully unlocked the door. Before entering, they listened for noises, but all they could hear was the rain outside, drumming loudly on the building's tile roof.

Elisabet felt a chill of fear as she entered the apartment. Once again, she had the overwhelming sensation she was being watched. "Let's not lock the door behind us tonight," she whispered. "Just in case we have to leave in a hurry."

"I wish we could leave now," Marie whispered back. "Let's check everything."

The girls examined both rooms until they were sure there was no hidden intruder. Then they started hunting for anything that might refer to a baby or a manger. They looked through the titles of all the books. They checked the drawers in the bedroom in hopes they might find a baby's swaddling clothes. They even reexamined the statue of the Madonna. They searched for almost three hours. But they found nothing.

Hot, tired, and frustrated, Elisabet opened the French windows for a few minutes. The street looked deserted. It was raining harder than ever now, and the wooden signs outside were creaking and swinging in the wind. As she stared out at the street, Elisabet kept thinking about the passage from Luke: "And this shall be a sign unto you; Ye shall find the babe wrapped in swaddling clothes, lying in a manger."

Suddenly, she had an idea. "Maybe my uncle wasn't talking about a baby," she exclaimed, pointing outside. "Maybe he meant a sign!"

Marie stepped up to the window and peered outside. "It is possible," she said. "It is one place no one has looked."

Together, the two girls hurried outside onto the tiny balcony. The rain slashed down at them, and the wind whipped their hair. Kneeling on the wet balcony floor, they were able to reach through the railing and unhook the Horn of Plenty's sign from its pole. The wooden sign was almost three feet long and heavier than they expected. It took all their combined strength to lift it over the railing and maneuver it in through the French windows.

"Monsieur DuMaurier made this sign himself, and he was very proud of it," Marie said as they laid the dripping sign on the floor by the open French windows. They examined it closely by candlelight. It was a hollow, painted wooden cornucopia, filled with carved wooden breads, cakes, and pastries. The two girls peered at the sign from all angles and poked inside between the carved, painted foods. All they could find were dirt and a few bird droppings.

Elisabet's heart felt heavy with disappointment, but she was determined not to give up. "I wish we had more light," she said. "I want to see farther back inside the horn."

Marie fetched a small mirror from Madame DuMaurier's bedroom. "Here," she said. "This should help."

They focused the light so it shone into the horn. "Look!" Elisabet exclaimed. "Way in the back—there's something there."

Marie grabbed a letter opener from a drawer. With growing excitement, the two girls used the opener's long blade to maneuver a thin leather pouch from the horn.

"Merciful saints!" Marie whispered.

Elisabet's hands trembled as she carefully opened the envelope-shaped pouch. Together, she and Marie unfolded a large, finely detailed, hand-drawn map titled:

A Guide to the Bayous and Swamps Surrounding New Orleans
By Henri DuMaurier

"We found it!" the two girls whooped. They hugged each other and danced around the room with joy. "We found it!"

Suddenly, they heard a harsh laugh from the doorway. Startled, they looked up to see Lucas McCain standing in the door. "Now," he rasped, "you can give it to me!"

CHAPTER 12
ESCAPE INTO THE STORM

 M cCain advanced upon the girls, a long knife held threateningly in his hand. Elisabet remained rooted in place in the middle of the parlor, her eyes fixed on the knife's wickedly sharp blade. Marie retreated toward the French windows, where the map still lay on the floor.

The big man ignored Elisabet and lumbered toward the map. His hands and face were filthy, and he smelled as if he had been drinking. "Well, thank you, girls," he said in a self-satisfied tone. "I had me a look-see through here the other night and I couldn't find nothing. Now it seems like you've gone and done my work for me!"

Elisabet and Marie glanced at each other, the same thought flashing through their minds: *It was Lucas McCain that we heard!*

Marie continued to back toward the map. "How did you get in here?" she asked. "The outside doors were locked."

"Ha, ha!" McCain's laugh rumbled. "You think little bitty locks like they got on them doors is enough to stop old Lucas McCain? Picking them locks was easier than cracking pecans! And tonight you girls was kind enough to leave the door up here open for me. Right thoughtful of you."

"You've been watching us, haven't you?" said Elisabet.

"I saw you girls up here one night and I knew you was looking around same as me. So I figured that instead of hunting myself, I'd let you be the hounds and sniff out that there map for me," said McCain.

"I've been watching you every night," he added with a mean smile. "Tonight when I saw you pull in that sign and then jump up and down, all happy-like, I knew you'd found the map." His expression hardened. "Now hand it over to me."

Marie slowly leaned down to pick up the map, and as she did, her eyes met Elisabet's. *She's stalling for time*, Elisabet realized. Elisabet remembered the heavy rolling pin they had brought with them. She was sorry they had left it back in the bedroom; it was useless there. Besides, what could two girls with a rolling pin do against McCain and his vicious knife? She knew Marie must have some other plan in mind. But what?

Elisabet watched her friend carefully as Marie picked up the map and showed it to McCain.

"Look, *monsieur*, this is not the map you wanted. It is

not a treasure map at all. It is just a map of the area around our city, a guide to the bayous. See? That is all."

McCain squinted at the map. His lips curved. "That's all the treasure I need right there, girl. I've heard tell them Brits will pay top money for a map like that. So why don't you just fold it up nice and give it to me. That way no one will get hurt."

As McCain fingered his long knife, Marie caught Elisabet's eye. Then she looked pointedly at the door. Elisabet took the hint and started to edge toward the parlor door. Marie began to fold the map slowly and painstakingly.

"Hurry up there, girl," McCain demanded. "I ain't got all night."

Marie managed to look innocent and surprised. "*Oui, monsieur!* I thought that because of the rain"—and here she looked behind herself at the violent storm raging outside the open French windows—"you would want me to put the map back in its pouch. But if you do not . . ." She offered the map to McCain.

The big man grunted. "Of course I want you to put the map in the pouch. Just be quick about it."

Elisabet continued to edge toward the door while Marie fussed over the map, getting the corners just so, then fitting it all neatly into the leather pouch. McCain towered over Marie, tapping his foot impatiently.

"All right," he said as Marie closed the pouch. "It's done. Now give it!"

"As you wish, sir," Marie replied respectfully. For a moment Elisabet was confused. Was her friend just going to hand the map over? Marie gave the big man her sweetest smile and stood up with the map pouch in her hand. But when McCain stepped forward, Marie suddenly turned. With a swift, powerful throw, she flung the pouch out the open French windows behind her.

"*Elisabet, get it!*" she screamed to her friend. Then she quickly blew out the candle the girls had used to illuminate the sign. The room was now in darkness.

Elisabet, who had maneuvered herself within a few feet of the door, took off down the stairs.

McCain shouted curses as he abandoned Marie and started off in pursuit of Elisabet. "I'll get you and I'll make you pay," he screamed. McCain, however, did not see the heavy wooden Horn of Plenty sign that lay across his path. He tripped over the sign and fell with a loud crash.

As McCain struggled to get to his feet, Elisabet flew down the stairs. The bakery shop was pitch-black, but Elisabet had spent so much time waiting on customers that she knew the layout of the shop by heart. She quickly threaded through the maze of little tables and chairs and escaped through the front door, which McCain had left unlocked.

Once on the street, she had a moment of panic. Where could the pouch have landed? The night was so dark and rainy it was almost impossible to see anything.

How could she find a thin leather pouch on the muddy streets? She could now hear McCain pounding down the narrow steps. He was yelling threats while Marie stood on the balcony screaming for help.

As she heard McCain stumble and crash his way through the dark bakery, Elisabet almost gave up hope of finding the pouch. He would reach her in just a few seconds. . . . Suddenly, she felt something slippery under her bare foot. She reached down. The pouch! She grabbed it and started running up the street.

It was none too soon. McCain almost caught up to her as she turned the corner, but he slipped in the mud and fell again. Elisabet sprinted and was able to put half a block between herself and the heavy man. Yet no matter how fast she ran, McCain kept following, cursing and threatening what he would do when he caught up with her.

Elisabet screamed for help as she ran. But the storm was so violent there was no one on the street to come to her aid. She knew the people inside their shuttered homes could not hear her cries above the howling wind and pounding rain. *Perhaps if I go far enough, I'll find someone who can help me*, she thought.

Driven by terror, Elisabet ran faster than she had ever run before. Yet after a few blocks, she felt herself tiring. Her long skirt, growing heavy from the rain, weighed her down, and her heart was beating so hard she thought it would burst.

Elisabet's hopes rose when she glimpsed the outline of a man on horseback just ahead. She was about to scream again for help when she saw it was not a man at all, but a statue. She had not paid attention to where she was going, but now she realized her instincts had taken her back to the Rue du Chevalier. *Please, please, let me reach Mr. Robinson's house*, she prayed.

She used her last burst of energy to turn the corner by the statue and sprint down the Rue du Chevalier. But it wasn't quite enough. As she ran, she could hear McCain's heavy breathing just a few steps behind her. He was gaining on her. She was almost in front of number seven when McCain leaped forward and caught her by the shoulder. He jerked her off balance, and she tumbled into the muddy street.

"Mr. Robinson!" she cried as she fell, trying hard to be heard above the wind and the rain. "*Mr. Robinson!*"

Elisabet struggled against McCain, but the big man overpowered her and snatched the pouch out of her grasp.

"I'll teach you to mess with Lucas McCain," he growled. He drew back his hand to slap her face.

Elisabet turned her head and closed her eyes. But the expected blow never came. Instead, she heard the loud howling of large, angry dogs. McCain cursed, then let go of her and staggered back.

Opening her eyes, she saw Mr. Robinson's dogs, Brutus and Caesar, jumping on McCain and snapping at his throat. *Arooooooooo!* bayed the angry dogs. *Arooooooo!*

Suddenly, two of the biggest, ugliest men Elisabet had ever seen ran up. One of the men had a long mustache and massive, hulking shoulders. The other man had a large gold ring through his nose.

Oh, no, Elisabet thought. *These men must work for McCain!*

The man with the nose ring gestured at the dogs. "Shut your traps!" he commanded. Then he twisted McCain's arm behind his back and held a knife to McCain's throat.

Brutus and Caesar stopped barking but kept up a low, menacing growl. They stood watching McCain with their teeth bared, ridges of fur standing up on their backs, and all their muscles ready for attack.

"Whatsa matter?" McCain sputtered as he looked fearfully from the threatening dogs to the two other men. "This ain't got nothing to do with you. This girl stole something from me and I was just—"

"Be quiet!" Nose Ring commanded, tightening his grip. He turned to Elisabet. "Why you been out here yelling for Mr. Robinson?"

"Mr. Robinson's my friend," Elisabet declared. She glared at McCain as she rose to her feet. "And I wasn't stealing anything. This man was stealing from me."

The man with the mustache and Nose Ring exchanged glances. "Go inside," Mustache ordered. "We'll let the boss decide."

Elisabet, taking care to keep as much distance as

possible between herself and McCain, followed Mustache into Mr. Robinson's house. McCain and Nose Ring trailed behind, with the watchful Caesar and Brutus at their heels.

From the outside, the house seemed dark and quiet. When they stepped inside, however, Elisabet saw that the walnut-paneled parlor was bright with candlelight, even though it was well past midnight. The room was elegant, with dark-blue velvet drapes over the windows, and chairs covered with matching blue velvet.

Mr. Robinson was sitting at a marble-topped table with a handsome gentleman in a well-tailored black suit. When the group walked in, he stood up in surprise. "Elisabet!" he exclaimed. "What in heaven's name are you doing here?"

"We looked to see what them dogs was howling about and we found these two outside," Mustache reported. He gestured at McCain. "He was fixing to beat this girl up, but the dogs got 'im first."

Nose Ring held up the leather pouch he had taken from McCain. "They was fighting over this."

Elisabet grabbed the pouch. "That's my uncle's map," she told Mr. Robinson, holding the pouch close to her body. "Marie and I found it tonight. Mr. McCain was trying to take it away from me."

Mr. Robinson turned to his guest. "This is the girl I mentioned to you earlier, Captain Holder's daughter."

McCain was staring at Mr. Robinson's guest. "I didn't

know *you* was in on this," McCain stammered, his face white with fear. "If I'd known, I'd never have—"

"Silence!" the guest commanded. "You robbed this young girl, then tried to beat her, eh? You're beneath contempt."

The guest stood up, his dark eyes flashing. He was just above medium height, slim but powerfully built. Although his voice was not loud, it carried unmistakable authority. He gestured at McCain. "Take him away," he ordered Nose Ring. "I'll deal with him later."

Nose Ring nodded and shoved the protesting McCain out of the room. Mustache followed, closing the parlor door behind him.

As soon as the door was shut, Mr. Robinson's guest bowed to Elisabet. "I am delighted to meet you, Miss Holder," he said. He gallantly pulled out a chair for Elisabet. "Won't you join us?"

CHAPTER 13
A MYSTERIOUS MEETING

Elisabet looked at the velvet chair and was suddenly aware of her wet, muddy clothes. "Thank you, but no—I wouldn't want to get mud on the chair."

The guest slipped off his elegant black suit coat and draped it over Elisabet's shoulders. It smelled of pipe tobacco, and it was so long that it fell beneath her knees. "There," he said with a smile. "That should take care of the chair and perhaps keep you from getting a chill."

Reluctantly, Elisabet sat down at the table. Brutus and Caesar curled up at her feet. A silver coffee service was already set up, and Mr. Robinson poured her a cup of coffee, which he mixed generously with hot milk.

"Drink this," he instructed her.

She took a sip of the hot coffee. It warmed her and helped revive her spirits. "Thank you," she said.

"Now, why don't you tell us what this is all about?"

Mr. Robinson encouraged her.

Elisabet looked questioningly at the guest and then back at Mr. Robinson. Mr. Robinson nodded reassuringly. "You may speak freely, Elisabet," he told her. "This gentleman is a friend of mine, and I have already spoken to him of your problems."

"Very well," said Elisabet. Between sips of coffee, she recounted the evening's adventures, beginning with the discovery of the map and ending with her struggles against McCain.

"I'm so glad you heard my screams," she told Mr. Robinson. "I didn't know what Mr. McCain was going to do to me."

Mr. Robinson smiled, then nodded at Brutus and Caesar. "You can credit the dogs for your rescue," he said. "They were the ones who heard you. Dogs don't forget their friends, you know."

At the word "dogs," Brutus and Caesar thumped their tails. Elisabet rubbed their heads. "Good dogs," she murmured. "Good dogs!"

"What about the map?" Mr. Robinson asked. "What does it show?"

"I don't know," Elisabet confessed. "We had only just opened it when Mr. McCain arrived. Here it is." She carefully removed the map from its muddy pouch and spread it on the table.

Heart pounding, she watched Mr. Robinson and his

guest as they examined Uncle Henri's map. Their faces showed little emotion. "Is it valuable?" she asked at last. "Is it worth enough to pay for my father's ransom?"

The guest looked at her sharply. "The British might pay a good deal for a map like this," he said. "It is the most accurate, detailed map of the bayous I've ever seen." He paused. "Would you like me to arrange a sale?"

"No!" Elisabet exclaimed. "I could never sell it to the British. Ever!"

The guest continued to study her closely. He leaned toward her. "What if it bought your father's freedom? Would you sell it to the British for that?"

Elisabet thought of Papa, a helpless prisoner aboard the British ship. If this piece of paper could free him, then perhaps . . .

Then she caught sight of herself in the large mirror that hung by the table. She looked very dirty, with straggly red hair, smudged face, and a muddy dress. But her eyes were her father's eyes—clear brown, with just a fleck of green. *I'm still Captain John Holder's daughter*, she told herself, *and Papa wouldn't sell out to the British for anything.*

"I want my father's freedom," she told the guest firmly. "But I won't sell to the British. Not for anything!"

The guest leaned back in his chair, and Elisabet noticed he seemed pleased with her answer. "You could sell this map to the governor of New Orleans. He might give you as much as one thousand dollars for it," the guest said. "Or you could sell it to me. I'll give you a thousand dollars, too, and I'll also help you get your father back."

"One thousand dollars is not enough to buy my father's freedom," Elisabet protested. "That pirate Jean Lafitte told Mr. Robinson it would cost three thousand dollars."

"Lafitte is not a pirate," the guest corrected her abruptly. "He is a privateer and a loyal American citizen."

"But could you help free my father without selling the map to the British?"

The handsome guest leaned back in his chair. "Yes, I believe it can be done," he said. "And do not worry yourself. Your map will not be used to help the British."

Elisabet looked at Mr. Robinson. "My friend is a man of honor, Elisabet," he assured her. "You may believe what he says."

But Elisabet was not convinced. "What about Mr. McCain?" she asked. "He knows I have the map. He will come after me."

"Do not worry about Monsieur McCain," the guest replied. "He will bother you no more."

"How can I be sure?" she persisted.

"You can be very sure," Mr. Robinson said firmly.

She took a deep breath. She felt as if she were about to dive into a deep, cold lake with no idea of where the bottom was. "Very well," she told the guest at last. "The map is yours as long as you promise never to let the British have it."

"You have my word I will not do anything to aid the British," the guest assured her.

He reached beneath the table and pulled out a heavy leather case. Elisabet watched in amazement as he counted out ten piles of gold coins, each pile worth one hundred dollars.

"Here is one thousand dollars," the guest said after all the coins were assembled on the table. He put the gold in a leather bag and handed it to Elisabet. "It's yours."

Never before in her life had Elisabet held so much money. And after being so recently chased through the streets by Lucas McCain, she was not at all sure she wanted to walk home with a bag full of gold.

"Is it safe for me to take this much money with me?" she asked Mr. Robinson.

"I'm sure an escort can be arranged," he replied, with a glance at his guest.

"It will be our pleasure," the guest agreed. He gave a low whistle, and Nose Ring appeared at the door.

"Yes, boss?"

"You men escort Miss Holder to her home," the guest told Nose Ring. "And see that she arrives there safely, you understand?"

"Yes, boss."

"What about your coat?" Elisabet asked the guest, looking down at the now-muddy suit coat.

"Keep it," the guest said. "I have others."

Elisabet patted the dogs good-bye and said farewell to Mr. Robinson and his guest. "Good-bye, Elisabet, and do not worry," Mr. Robinson said.

Yet she could not help but worry. Just as she was walking out of the parlor, she turned back to the guest. "When will I hear word of my father?" she asked.

"Soon," he said. "Trust me."

Elisabet, however, wondered if she had already trusted too much. She walked out into the night, holding tight to the bag of gold coins. Mustache and Nose Ring walked silently behind her. The rain had stopped. By the time Elisabet reached the Horn of Plenty, birds were chirping and the first light of dawn was beginning to brighten the eastern horizon.

"Here is my home," she told the men.

"We'll wait till you're in," Nose Ring grunted.

The two men stood in the shadows while Elisabet knocked loudly on the bakery door. In just a few seconds, a tearful Marie appeared on the doorstep.

"Thank the Lord you are all right!" she exclaimed. She hugged Elisabet tightly and pulled her inside the shop. Mustache and Nose Ring quietly disappeared down the street.

Claude and Raoul were right behind Marie. "We've been worried about you," said Claude, enveloping Elisabet in a warm hug. "Marie came to my home and told me what happened."

"Then they got me up," said Raoul. "We've been up all night looking everywhere for you," he grumbled, but he too seemed glad to see her.

Her three friends took Elisabet back to the kitchen. She noticed there was no fire in the oven and no smell of fresh-baked bread. *They stopped their work just to look for me*, she thought, and tears came to her eyes.

Marie saw the tears and misinterpreted them. "You *are* all right, aren't you?" she asked fearfully. "Did McCain hurt you?"

"I'm fine," Elisabet reassured her. Quickly, she told them everything that had happened. "I hope I did the right thing in selling the map," she said, looking anxiously at Marie. "I know we found it together, and it was not really mine to sell, but—"

"But you did what you thought was best for your father," Marie finished for her. "Don't worry. Monsieur DuMaurier never would have wanted McCain or the British to get the map."

"Where is the money?" Raoul asked eagerly.

"Here," said Elisabet, pulling out the heavy bag of coins.

"*Sacrebleu!*" exclaimed Raoul, reaching out to touch the gold.

Claude took charge. "I will lock the gold in the safe until Madame DuMaurier returns home," he said, picking up the bag. "She will decide how the reward should be divided."

"The only reward I want is to get Papa back," Elisabet said. She took off the suit coat that Mr. Robinson's guest had given her and put her head down on the kitchen table. Suddenly, she was terribly tired. If only she could rest for just a few minutes. . . .

Claude picked up the elegant coat and looked inside it. "Elisabet," he asked, "what exactly did this guest of Mr. Robinson's look like?"

Elisabet raised her head. "Medium height, but strong," she told Claude. "Dark hair and eyes, handsome, very polite but somehow . . ." She searched for a word. "Somehow he seemed dangerous, too. At least Lucas McCain seemed afraid of him, and the men called him 'Boss.' I suppose he's a lawyer like Mr. Robinson, and Mr. McCain was afraid he'd be arrested."

Claude shook his head. "I do not think so," he said. He held up the coat. Monogrammed on the inside of the jacket were the letters *J L.* "I'd wager that your mysterious guest was Jean Lafitte himself."

Elisabet sat up straight in her chair. "Oh, no! The pirate? I've given my uncle's map to a pirate?" She looked at the black coat with sudden horror. *How could she ever have trusted her father's fate to a pirate?*

"Jean Lafitte may be an outlaw, but he is known as a man of his word," Claude reassured her. "If anyone can help your father, he can."

Claude glanced outside at the brightening sky. "Our

first customers will be here soon," he said. "Go clean yourself and get some rest. We will try to let you sleep as long
as possible."

Elisabet dragged herself upstairs. Before drifting off to
sleep she sent a silent prayer to her father. *Forgive me, Papa.
I tried my best, but I think I trusted the wrong man.*

CHAPTER 14
A PIRATE'S PROMISE

When Elisabet finally awakened, the sun was low on the horizon. It was late afternoon! She put on a clean work shift and hurried downstairs to the bakery.

Marie greeted her with a grin. "There you are, sleepyhead," she said. "You feel better now, *non?*"

"I feel much better, but I'm so sorry I slept through the whole day. How did you manage in the shop without me?"

"Raoul helped me whenever he had a chance. He acts as if he does not care about anyone, but in truth he does. We all decided it was better for you to rest today."

"Thank you," Elisabet said, giving her friend a hug. "Now you go upstairs and take a rest until supper. I'll take care of things here."

"Are you sure?" Marie said doubtfully. "The bakery is quiet now, but later—"

"Later it will be all right, too," Elisabet assured her.

"I'll even arrange the shelves properly. I promise."

Marie smiled. "Very well. I am a little tired," she admitted, and slowly climbed upstairs.

Elisabet reflected that Marie, Claude, and Raoul had all gone without sleep the previous night, but they had sacrificed to let her rest during the day. *They are true friends*, she thought. *I only wish Papa could meet them.*

During the next few days, life at the Horn of Plenty gradually settled back into its normal routine. Now that the "ghost" was gone, the girls slept well at night. And Raoul confessed to Claude that he had been the ghost that the neighbors had seen.

"I thought you knew more about the ghost than you were willing to admit," Claude said with a smile. Then he turned to Elisabet and Marie. "And by the way, you girls can keep that extra rolling pin upstairs as long as you want."

So Claude had known all along that they had taken the rolling pin for protection during the nights! Both girls laughed.

"But Claude, did you suspect Monsieur McCain, too?" Marie asked. "Did you know he was watching us?"

Claude's face clouded. "No. I wish I had known. I thought he was all talk. As it was . . . well, I am glad no one got hurt."

Elisabet shivered as she remembered the terror of the chase through the stormy New Orleans night. "Do you think Lucas McCain will ever come back here?"

"*Non*," Claude said firmly. "Didn't you say that Monsieur Lafitte promised to take care of McCain?"

"Yes," Elisabet said.

"Then he will most certainly do so. Think no more about it."

Elisabet breathed a sigh of relief. Claude's words enabled her finally to put McCain out of her mind for good. *But what about Papa?* she thought. *Mr. Lafitte also promised to help him, and so far there's been no word of Papa at all.*

Each day, Elisabet wondered whether she would get news of her father. But the days passed, and still she heard nothing. Claude counseled patience. "These things take time," he told her. "Have faith."

But for Elisabet the wait was agonizing. One day, more than a week after her meeting with Jean Lafitte and Mr. Robinson, she overheard a conversation between two customers in the bakery. They said the government planned to raid Jean Lafitte's island, Grande Terre.

"The governor has had enough of Jean Lafitte," a blond man was saying. "He sent the navy down to Grande Terre yesterday. They are going to take over that island and teach that pirate a lesson."

"Do you really think it'll be that easy?" asked his companion, an older man.

"Of course," said the younger man. "Lafitte is nothing but an outlaw. This time, we'll show him who is boss."

"I would not be so sure," the older man cautioned. "He is a crafty devil."

Pirate! Outlaw! Crafty devil! The words went straight to Elisabet's heart. This was the man she had trusted to save her father! And now, perhaps Jean Lafitte's whole island would be taken over by the government. If that was true, he might not be able to help Papa even if he wanted to. What would happen then?

For the first time in her life, Elisabet found herself praying for a pirate. *Please do not let anything happen to Mr. Lafitte,* she prayed silently. *Papa's life may depend on him.*

Elisabet desperately hoped for news of her father from Mr. Robinson, but the lawyer never visited. Finally, Claude, knowing how anxious she was, permitted her to go to Mr. Robinson's house.

"Raoul must deliver some cakes in that neighborhood this afternoon," Claude told her. "You may go with him."

When Raoul was ready to go on his errand, Elisabet put on her best dress and bonnet and accompanied him into the narrow streets. It was midafternoon, bright and sunny, and everywhere Elisabet looked she saw blooming shrubs and window boxes full of bright flowers. When they reached the statue at the corner of the Rue du Chevalier, she pointed out Mr. Robinson's house to Raoul.

"There it is," she said, pointing to the imposing brick and stucco home, "number seven."

"Very well." Raoul nodded. "I must take these cakes down to a house on the next street. I will meet you back at this statue."

They parted company, and Elisabet walked up to the front door of Mr. Robinson's house alone. She thought back to the night more than a week ago when she had arrived at the house muddy and terrified. How different everything looked now in the bright light of day!

As soon as she let the brass door knocker fall, she heard Brutus and Caesar inside baying. *Arooooo! Aroooo!* The housekeeper opened the door, and the dogs greeted Elisabet with thumping tails and little jumps of excitement. The housekeeper smiled pleasantly, but when Elisabet asked to see Mr. Robinson, she shook her head.

"I'm sorry, dear, but he is out of town. I don't know when he'll be back."

Out of town! Elisabet's spirits sank. "Did he leave a message for Elisabet Holder?"

The housekeeper shook her head. "None, child."

Dejected, Elisabet patted Brutus and Caesar and slowly returned to the statue to wait for Raoul. When he arrived, he could tell from Elisabet's face that the visit had gone badly. Tactfully, he said nothing, and the two walked back to the bakery together in silence.

They found Marie eagerly waiting for them. "We have good news!" she announced with a smile.

"What! Where is he? Where is Papa?" Elisabet cried.

Marie's face fell. "No, I am sorry, Elisabet, I didn't mean to raise your hopes. It is not about your papa at all. It is about Madame DuMaurier. We got a letter from her today. Her daughter is better, and Madame DuMaurier should be coming home in a week or so."

"Oh," Elisabet said, trying not to sound as disappointed as she felt. "That is good news, too."

Four more days passed without word of her father or the *Sophie*. Then late one afternoon, Raoul returned to the bakery after buying supplies at the market. "Did you hear any news of the *Sophie*?" Elisabet asked him. "Any news at all?"

Raoul avoided her eyes. "Ah, you cannot believe every-thing you hear, you know."

"What?" Elisabet demanded, her throat tight with anxiety. "You heard something—now tell me!"

Reluctantly, Raoul told her the news: the American navy had succeeded in invading Lafitte's island of Grande Terre. Lafitte himself had escaped, along with most of his ships. But some of his ships and cannons were captured. A few dozen of his men were taken prisoner, and many of the buildings on the island had been burned to the ground.

"Oh, no," Elisabet cried. "Why did the navy have to

attack Jean Lafitte now—just as he was going to help my father?"

"The rumor is, the British made a deal with Lafitte," Raoul explained, looking down at the floor. "People are saying the British are going to get the rest of their fleet and come back to invade us. The governor did not want Lafitte to help the British, so he ordered the navy to destroy Grande Terre." Raoul paused. "I am sorry, Elisabet."

Lafitte had made a deal with the British! Elisabet was heartsick. After Raoul went back to work in the kitchen, she stood for a long time in the empty bakery. She stared at the shelves of breads and pastries, with tears running down her cheeks. She knew now that she had been betrayed by the pirate Lafitte. All her work to find the map had only ended in helping the British. The bell on the front door jangled, but Elisabet didn't even turn around as she heard footsteps on the brick floor.

I hope this is not Caroline and her father, she thought as she wiped her wet cheeks with her sleeve and prepared to face her customers. *I don't think I can bear to wait on them today.*

Suddenly, she heard a familiar deep voice say, "The food here looks good, but what I'd really like is some Boston brown bread."

"Papa!" she cried in astonishment. Then she ran to her father's arms. "Oh, Papa!"

He looked thin, tired, and pale, but he had the same

smile that she had cherished in her heart all the months they were apart. Elisabet held him as if she would never let him go.

"Oh, but Papa," she finally asked, "how did you get free?"

Captain Holder smiled down at her. "I owe my freedom to my brave daughter," he said. "Monsieur Lafitte traded with the British—your map for my freedom."

"Oh, no!" Elisabet's face crumpled and her shoulders slumped. "I'm sorry, Papa. He *promised* me he wouldn't sell the map to the British. I never meant them to have it."

"Don't worry," her father comforted her. He glanced around the empty bakery, then whispered, "Monsieur Lafitte warned me you might be upset. He said to tell you a little secret: the map he sold the British was actually a copy of DuMaurier's. When Monsieur Lafitte had the copy made, he introduced a few changes here and there. If the British ever try to use the map to navigate by, they'll be lost in the bayous for sure."

Elisabet felt as if a pile of stones had been taken off her shoulders. She hugged her father even tighter. "I am so glad he kept his promise!"

Captain Holder scowled. "That is more than I can say for that skunk of a lawyer I have in Boston."

"Mr. Gruber?" Elisabet asked in surprise. "Why, he was the one who sent me here." She paused. "I'm sorry, Papa, but he had to sell everything we owned to pay for your cargo that was lost."

Captain Holder's face grew even darker. "I know. I heard the story from your friend Mr. Robinson. But it's a pack of lies. There was plenty of insurance on that cargo, and Gruber knew it. He cheated us, plain and simple, and took all the money for himself. When we get back to Boston, I am going to get back every penny—and more."

Back to Boston! It was Elisabet's dream come true. But then she remembered something.

"Papa," she said, taking her father by the hand. "There are some people you must meet."

She led her father into the kitchen. "Papa, these are my good friends, Claude and Raoul," she said. Then she turned to the surprised Marie. "And this is my 'cousin,' Marie."

"I am very pleased to meet you all," Captain Holder said warmly. Then he turned to Claude. "And thank you for taking care of my daughter."

"She took good care of herself," said Claude, smiling. "She has worked hard here."

"My little Elisabet, a hard worker," said Captain Holder, looking at his barefoot daughter in her work shift. "It does not seem possible."

Elisabet smiled, a little embarrassed. "Marie taught me everything, Papa. At first, I did not want to learn, but she taught me anyway. It was hard, much harder than school ever was."

A sudden thought occurred to Elisabet. She reached

up and whispered something in her father's ear. He looked over at Marie, then smiled at his daughter. "Well, why don't you ask her?"

"Marie," said Elisabet excitedly. "Why don't you come back to Boston with me? We could be like sisters, and we could go to school together!"

Claude and Raoul looked at Marie and waited for her answer. She did not hesitate. "Thank you, but no. This is my home." She gestured at the kitchen. "It is all the school I ever wanted. Here, I can learn how to run a bakery. I could not learn that in your Boston school."

"Are you sure?" asked Elisabet, disappointed.

"Very sure," said Marie. "But we can write to each other and perhaps even visit. I would like to see your Boston someday."

"It is too cold up there," Raoul interjected. "I hear that in the winter even the ocean freezes. You do not want to go there!"

Claude smiled. "I think you would like to keep Marie here, wouldn't you, Raoul?" The skinny boy blushed, and Claude turned to Elisabet's father. "When do you plan to return to Boston, *monsieur*?"

"As soon as we can get a ship out," Captain Holder replied. "Probably a week or so."

It was exactly a week before Elisabet and her father found themselves on the deck of a ship, sailing down the Mississippi River. Aunt Augustine had arrived back in New Orleans just the day before they left. Now she, Marie, Claude, and Raoul were all standing on the levee, waving good-bye to the ship. Elisabet waved back, tears in her eyes.

"Nothing was the way I expected it would be," said Elisabet, "but they were all kind to me—even when I didn't deserve it."

"They were good friends," her father agreed, "and when I regain my fortune, I would like to reward them. I have talked with your aunt about Marie's dream of some-day owning the bakery. I think we will be able to arrange something."

"Oh, Papa," Elisabet said, "that would be wonderful! Marie worked so hard to help me find Uncle Henri's map. We both thought it would lead to treasure, but of course we never found any treasure, just the map."

"What you discovered was more important than treasure, Elisa," said Captain Holder, as he looked lovingly at his daughter. "You found new friends and family—what could be more valuable than that?"

Then Captain Holder rummaged in his pocket. "By the way," he said, "Marie asked me to give you this when we were on board ship. Here you are."

He handed Elisabet a tiny package wrapped in brown

paper. She opened it eagerly. It was a two-inch square of tattered yellow blanket with a note attached. "Keep this and think of me," the note read. "Your friend, forever, Marie."

A Peek into the Past

LOOKING BACK: 1814

In 1814, American girls like Elisabet Holder were proud of their country's freedom. They knew that American patriots had fought for independence from Great Britain and won the American Revolution in 1783.

But even after the Revolution ended, Great Britain treated the United States more like a possession than an independent country. After Great Britain went to war against France in 1803, the situation got worse. To prevent Americans from trading with the French, the British navy stopped American ships at sea and stole their cargo. Even worse, they captured American sailors—like Elisabet's father—and forced, or *impressed,* them into the British navy.

Americans were outraged. The United States declared a "Second War of Independence" against Great Britain in 1812.

What is now called the War of 1812 began badly for the United States. Inexperienced American troops lost battles along the Great Lakes, in Canada, and at sea. In August 1814, the

Throughout the early 1800s, American sailors were captured at sea and forced to work in the British navy.

British invaded Washington, D.C. They captured the nation's capital and burned the White House to the ground.

Soon after, Americans won a major victory at Baltimore, Maryland. Relieved to see the United States flag still flying when the battle ended, a lawyer and poet named Francis Scott Key wrote "The Star-Spangled Banner." It later became the national anthem.

Finally, the British decided to attack New Orleans. In 1814, farmers in the middle part of the country sent their crops by river to New Orleans, where they were loaded onto ships and sailed down the Mississippi River to the Atlantic Ocean. The British knew that by capturing New Orleans, they could block one of America's most crucial trade routes.

British troops burned the White House in 1814. First Lady Dolley Madison refused to flee until she had saved important state papers.

But New Orleans was almost impossible to attack by surprise. It was surrounded by dangerous swamps and mazelike waterways called *bayous*. For help in capturing New Orleans, the British turned to the powerful pirate leader Jean Lafitte.

Unlike Elisabet and her family, who are fictional characters, Lafitte was a real person. He was a famous

A Louisiana bayou, surrounded by cypress swamp

privateer and the leader of Barataria—a stronghold of 1,000 pirates and smugglers on Grande Terre, an island near the mouth of the Mississippi. From Barataria, Lafitte's men attacked ships sailing in the Gulf of Mexico, took their cargo, then disappeared into the bayous.

In autumn 1814, at about the time Elisabet's story takes place, British officers from the ship *Sophie* tried to make a deal with Lafitte. They offered him wealth and power in exchange for his help in capturing New Orleans.

Lafitte pretended to consider the British offer, but he was loyal to his country. He told the New Orleans governor about the planned invasion. The governor, however, believed Lafitte was trying to trick him and ordered American forces to destroy Barataria.

Jean Lafitte

But as the British drew closer to New Orleans, American leaders realized Lafitte had been telling the truth and could provide supplies, skills, and manpower crucial to the city's defense. They decided to accept his help.

On January 8, 1815, a ragtag army of 5,000 frontiersmen, New Orleans militia, slaves, free African Americans, and pirates soundly defeated 9,000 experienced British soldiers at the Battle of New Orleans. The pirates fought so bravely that President James Madison granted them a full pardon for their earlier crimes.

Americans everywhere celebrated the great victory in New Orleans. Later, though, they discovered that a treaty ending the war had been signed in Europe on December 24, 1814. Because it took weeks for news to cross the Atlantic, neither side had known the War of 1812 was over before its biggest battle was fought.

The "Second War of Independence" was important because it proved America's determination to remain free. It also proved that Americans from different parts of the country and different ethnic backgrounds could work together to fight for their nation.

Nowhere was America's mix of cultures more evident than in New Orleans. Before the Louisiana Purchase made New Orleans part of the United States in 1803, the city had belonged first to France, then to Spain, then to France again. In 1814, many New Orleans residents still considered themselves French or Spanish, not American.

In 1803, France sold the Louisiana Territory, shown in gold, to the U.S. The painting shows the American flag flying in New Orleans for the first time, as the French flag is taken down.

But America was changing fast, and New Orleans — then the nation's sixth largest city — was changing with it. The city was a center for trade and a starting point for settlers heading west. German immigrants, Kentucky frontier families, Native Americans, African slaves, and free people of color from the West Indies all came to New Orleans. The city's international heritage was reflected in its French pastries, spicy African-style gumbos, tropical flowers, and shady Spanish courtyards, and in the languages heard on its streets.

A New Orleans courtyard today

To a New England girl like Elisabet, New Orleans probably would have seemed more foreign than American. It would also have been a shock for an upper-class girl like Elisabet to work in a bakery. In 1814, girls from wealthy families usually had private schooling and played with other upper-class girls. They practiced fancy needlework, but their servants did the real work.

In the early 1800s, only wealthy girls had much free time for study and play. Most middle-class American girls began learning skills such as cooking, sewing, and spinning by the age of six or seven. Their education in homemaking was considered as important as their schoolwork, and they were expected to spend much of their time helping their mothers.

Girls from poor families, and orphans like Marie, were often hired out to work at an early age. These girls usually had little or no formal education. Laws did not require children to attend school, and most schools were open only to children whose parents could afford tuition.

Upper-class girls practiced fancy stitchery and had elegant toys like this doll, which belonged to a shipmaster's daughter in 1812.

Some towns, however, offered small public or charity schools, and some churches taught the poor. A girl like Marie who attended such a school might become the first woman in her family ever to learn to write her name or to read a book.

A spelling lesson in a public school during the early 1800s

GLOSSARY OF FRENCH WORDS

au revoir *(oh reh-vwar)* —good-bye

banquette *(bahn-ket)* —the word used in New Orleans for a raised wooden sidewalk or boardwalk

beignets *(beh-nyay)* —sweet fried pastries that are a specialty in New Orleans

bien *(byen)* —good, all right

bienvenue *(byen-veh-noo)* —welcome

bonjour *(bohn-zhoor)* —hello

bonne nuit *(bun nwee)* —good night

bonsoir *(bohn-swahr)* —good evening

café au lait *(kah-feh oh leh)* —coffee mixed with hot milk

Grande Terre *(grahnd tehr)* —an island near the mouth of the Mississippi River

jolies fleurs *(zho-lee fler)* —pretty flowers

madame *(mah-dahm)* —Mrs. or madam

mademoiselle *(mahd-mwah-zel)* —miss

merci *(mehr-see)* —thank you

monsieur *(muh-syer)* —Mr. or sir

non *(nohn)* —no

oui *(wee)* —yes

par excellence *(pahr ek-seh-lahns)* —supreme, excellent

pardon *(pahr-dohn)* —excuse me

pirogue *(pee-rohg)* —a boat similar to a canoe

pistolettes *(pee-stoh-let)* — rolls whose name means "little pistol" because gentlemen sometimes ate them for breakfast before fighting a duel

Place d'Armes *(plahs dahrm)* — one of the main squares or plazas in New Orleans

roulés *(roo-lay)* — pastries made of rolled-out dough that is spread with filling and then rolled up

Rue du Chevalier *(roo doo sheh-vahl-yay)* — Street of the Horseman

sacrebleu *(sah-kreh-bluh)* — good heavens

très bien *(tray byen)* — very good

zut alors *(zoot ah-lor)* — darn it

About the Author

Sarah Masters Buckey grew up in New Jersey, where her favorite hobbies were swimming in the summer, sledding in the winter, and reading all year round. She loved to read so much that whenever her family packed their car for vacations, her mother would include a big bag of books just for her. As a writer, she has enjoyed living in different parts of the United States, including fifteen years in Texas. She now lives in New Hampshire's Upper Valley with her husband and their three children.

FREE CATALOGUE!

American Girl Gear is all about who you are today—smart, spirited, and ready for anything! Our catalogue is full of clothes and accessories that let you express yourself, with great styles for every occasion!

Send for your **free** catalogue, call **1-800-845-0005**, or visit our Web site at **www.americangirl.com**.

Send me a catalogue:

My name
_____

My address
_____

City _____ State _____ Zip 12567

My birth date: ____ / ____ / ____
                month day year

My e-mail address
_____

Send my friend a catalogue:

My friend's name
_____

Address
_____

City _____ State _____ Zip 12575

_____
Parent's signature

BUSINESS REPLY MAIL

FIRST-CLASS MAIL   PERMIT NO. 1137   MIDDLETON WI

POSTAGE WILL BE PAID BY ADDRESSEE

PO BOX 620497
MIDDLETON WI 53562-9940

NO POSTAGE
NECESSARY
IF MAILED
IN THE
UNITED STATES